I0646395

Queen of the Roller Derby

Joel Fel

RAH Press

ISBN # 9780989269353

ISBN # 0989269353

Kindle Edition 1993
Print Edition   2015

Chapter 1: Huey

The Voice of Humanity first rolled across the Green Hills of Earth at 6:18 P.M., Eastern Standard Time, January 31, 1993. "Rolled," of course, is a metaphor, since the Voice of Humanity had no wheels, and in any case the Green Hills of Earth were too craggy, bumpy and forested to roll across, even for the Voice of Humanity, even if it had wheels, which, of course, it didn't.

"Rolling" was a big metaphor for Humanity, with a long history. The Buffalo Bills

rolled over the rest of the American Football
Conference in the last decade of Old Humanity as
thunder rolled across the skies, the most popular
form of music invented by them was called "rock
and roll", and, all the while, Old Man River, he
just keep rolling along. No wheels for any of
these, either. Most of all, though, rolling was a
great metaphor because it turned out in the end
to be an important part of The Meaning of Life.

Humanity had always been concerned
with The Meaning of Life since Socrates and
Confucius first suggested life ought to have a
meaning, and Humanity could no more stop
wondering about The Meaning of Life than it
could spit on the back of its own neck.

I wasn't here when the Voice of Humanity
first rolled over the Green Hills of Earth, and, I
have to say, I didn't actually hear it myself. In
fact, it wasn't until my Uncle Hogg heard the
Voice rolling that anybody in Galaxy Central even
knew Humanity was alive. It didn't take but a
few minutes before Uncle Hogg thought I should
roll over to earth for a closer look. I wasn't much

interested in spending a couple of thousand years in the Boonies at just that moment, but then Uncle Hogg is the Boss, and so here I am.

My name is Roscoe, but of course "Roscoe" is just the closest I can come to saying my name in English. Some folks in Galaxy Central think "Bozo" is a closer translation, but it seems to me that Humanity might misunderstand that name. (There's still a big fight in Galaxy Central University about whether a name ought to be translated to be closest to what it *sounds like* or to what it *means*. I'm the first to admit my name *sounds* more like "Bozo" than "Roscoe" in English, but I have to insist that it doesn't *mean* anything even close to "Bozo" on Earth. Oh, well.)

What the Voice of Humanity said when it first rolled across the green hills of Earth was something pretty close to "Great Gosh Almighty!", but not everybody on Earth heard it that way. More than half the people in France will still swear it said "Sacre Bleu!", while their next door neighbors heard "Mon Dieu!" just as clearly. Jurgen Habermas listed three reasons why it had to have said "Gruss Gott!", although he did not hear the voice himself. The great totally post modern critic Thomas Newhouse wrote a brief but very popular essay that claimed it said "Holy Shit!"

As amazed as they were by the Voice of Humanity, people would probably have put it out of their minds quickly enough had it not been for the timing of the Voice. Why Humanity chose 6:18 PM, Eastern Standard Time, January 31, 1993 for its first words drove ordinary citizens to philosophy, and drove philosophers mad. By 1994, 62,340 citizens of the European Economic Community had joined the Durkheim League, which believed the world developed Collective Consciousness on Bastille Day AD 1992. The Durkheim League held further that Humanity had bided its time until the kickoff of the Super Bowl to announce its existence the largest possible audience. Really! I mean, if you're going to wait until the beginning of the Super Bowl so you can speak to 100 million people at once, wouldn't you say something someone could understand?

Now Humanity -- Huey -- is a pretty good friend of mine by now, and I can tell you that all this speculation is a lot of (pardon my French) pure bullshit. I mean, Great Gosh Almighty, do *you* remember what *you* said the first moment you were born?

Chapter 2: Curly

Dean "Curly" Kurland, the Dean of the Faculty of Social and Behavioral Sciences (FSBS) at the University at Buffalo was not himself a social or behavioral scientist. He was, in fact, a neuroscientist, and a Damn Fine one at that. He had published over 120 articles in scholarly journals, and had authored a Significant Textbook which was still in print.

As his promotion dossier revealed, he had made important contributions to the Neuron Doctrine, particularly for his research concerning the electrochemical processes involved in dendritic transfer of neural impulses (whatever that means). Dean Kurland was listed in *American Men and Woman in Science, Who's Who in the East, and Who's Who*. Three of his articles were discussed in *Science News*, and he had placed several small pieces in *Science*. He took great pride in the fact that, even though Dean, he continued an active research program. He was, as it were, a master of the synapse, and a man of great discipline.

He was also so far up to his neck in budget crises, legal difficulties and the ordinary dumb stuff that happens to Major Deans that he had pretty much lost track of himself and what he was doing. To make matters worse, he was horny as a hoot owl.

Deans were probably the most misunderstood and maligned members of Humanity's University faculties. Positioned as they were between the Provost or equivalent officer at the top end, and perhaps 20 or so Department Chairs who in no way considered the Dean their boss, supervisor or even peer, the Dean was often a lonely man. (There were woman deans, but you could grow weary looking for one. Alas, although the universities of the 1990's were the flowing fountain of Political Correctness, very few woman could be found in High Places there, and the only kind of women in good supply were students.)

Department Chairs were the first line officers in the field, and, for this and other reasons, were often unreasonable or even looney tunes. Chairs in the FSBS supervised between 8 and 50 faculty, none of whom believed they needed answer to anyone save posterity and The Discipline. Chairs looked to the Dean for virtually all their resources, and needed to convince him (see above paragraph concerning woman deans) that their needs were more urgent than their fellow chairs'. They felt hindered in this by the belief that no one outside their own discipline could understand what it was they did, or why it was important.

And so university faculty were about evenly divided on whether Deans were a necessary evil or an unnecessary evil. Assistant Deans were thought of as mice studying to be rats.

And this was a worse than usual time for Deans everywhere. With the economy still in the sewer after four years of bad budgets (the last two were Really Bad Budgets), only one or two of Curly's departments were in decent shape. Three faculty members were being investigated for sexual harassment, the Graduate Student Association was petitioning the Teamsters Union for a representation election, and 15 seniors who couldn't graduate because there weren't enough seats available in Communication Department classes had sued their Chair and Dean Kurland for Failure to Educate. This last issue was a might troublesome, because the total claim exceeded his Failure to Educate insurance by about $2.5 million.

Curly was more than a little worried about this suit, because he was clearly guilty and he knew it. The Communication Chair (who was beyond a doubt the looniest of all the tunes) had warned him in no uncertain terms that, with 350 undergraduate majors and only 8 faculty, Communication was stretched way too thin, and that a little minor matter like a fatal car crash or something could wipe out enough of the Communication Department faculty to make it impossible to service the existing student body. There was an implied contract with the 350 majors to provide them the opportunity to earn a degree, and, if the Dean admitted anyone else into that program while knowing he might not be able to keep his bargain, he was guilty as sin.

But Curly threw the dice, and assigned one of his precious seven new faculty lines into Sociology instead, and, sure enough if one of those godamn bozos didn't drive off the Rainbow

Bridge taking 25% of the Communication Faculty and 2 teaching assistants to a watery grave on the Canadian side of the Niagara River right next to the Maid of the Mist and 37 horrified passengers.

Dean Kurland went to the provost with his hat in his hand and explained the unfortunate demise of the Communication faculty and their graduate assistants, carefully avoiding the question of why the two men and their two female assistants were in Canada in the first place, and why they were returning drunk enough not to notice Niagara Falls.

The provost was sympathetic, but pointed out that friends and associates of the administration in Washington had stolen so much money in the Savings and Loan scandal that he was now required to put widows, orphans and terminal cancer patients out on the street. (The Provost deeply suspected that the deceased foursome had been trying to drink Canada Dry, but diplomatically said nothing.)

The dean understood the global situation, but opined that displacing just a few more widows and orphans could prevent something Really Serious from happening at UB, as he affectionately called the University at Buffalo. The provost wavered, but in the end he went with the widows and orphans, and Curly had to think of another way.

And the way he thought of was ... merger. The Communication Department had way too many students already in the pipeline, and not enough faculty to take care of them. The Sociology Department, on the other hand, had 50% more faculty and fewer than 1/3 as many students. And, Great Gosh Almighty, sociology was a *core discipline*. (Dean Kurland believed this meant that sociology was a more central or important subject than communication, but what it really meant was that sociology departments had got started in US universities about 50 years before communication departments, and so had a lot more friends.)

But even if sociology departments were thicker with the academic community, they were a Drug on the Market with students. Since the collapse of the Soviet Union, sociologists were the world's last remaining socialists, and whatever you might think about the Deeper Meaning of Sociological Theory, sociology degrees weren't popular in the business community in the Reagan-Bush era, particularly in the almost nonexistent job market of the early '90's.

And there was a peculiar image problem. Companies were willing, even eager, to admit they had a Communication Problem in their organization, and, in fact, tended to attribute almost everything that was wrong in their companies to Problems in Communication. To solve these problems, they were willing to hire bright young students trained in communication, and to hire faculty consultants from UB and elsewhere to help solve their Communication Problems. Faculty made friends as well as money in business, and a steady stream of bright young

faces   rolled   through   communication
departments all over the country to learn how to
solve some of these Communication Problems
themselves.

But no company had yet been discovered
that was willing to concede it had a (Yikes!)
Sociological Problem. So sociologists were a tad
short   of   undergraduate   majors   while
Communication Students were bustin' out all
over.

Eh, Voila, the solution struck Dean
Kurland like Niagara Falls in the rainy season:
the Sociology Department would mate with the
Communication Department, and make a big,
healthy Sociology Department with almost 20
faculty and over 400 majors -- a truly Big,
Powerful Department, a Big, Powerful *Central*
Department, a feather in Curly's cap. (Curly, as it
happened, was totally bald, as bald as a baby's
butt, which, along with the near rhyme it made
with Kurland, was why everyone called him
"Curly.")

Now, you might ask why the 350 students who wanted a degree in Communication would be satisfied with a degree in Sociology. And you might ask whether Communication faculty could teach Sociology courses and *vice versa*. Alas, you would never be a Dean.

In truth, Dean Kurland, as a Distinguished Neuroscientist, knew damn little about either sociology or communication, and, as a Real Scientist (physicists would be grumbling a bit, but, my God, you've got to let someone into the club, after all), Curly thought both sociology and communication were a kind of mindless mumbo-jumbo that ranked somewhere between Voodoo and the *National Enquirer*. (This was not what he said when he interviewed for the Deanship, but this job paid $115,000 a year back when a dollar really meant something!)

But, wherever they ranked, sociology ranked just a wee bit higher, and so the sociologists would be the husband in this marriage (see paragraph 4 of this chapter for a note on the status of women in the University).

Thus the communication department would surrender its name and identity evermore to take on the status of its new husband.

As it turned out, there was a fatal flaw in this courtship that ruined Dean Kurland's plans and almost ruined Dean Kurland. As it happened, the happy couple did not seem to love each other.

Chapter 3: Roscoe

This probably seems a bit disjointed to you, since there doesn't appear to be much connection between the Voice of Humanity rolling over the Green Hills of Earth and the mating ritual between the communication department and the sociology department at the University of Buffalo. There is, though, and it's plain enough.

Two people, Professor Lu Wi of the communication department and a computer programmer named DuMond play a key role in the Rolling of the Voice, and they haven't met as yet. In fact, if the communication department pledges its troth to the sociology department, Professor Lu Wi will almost certainly not teach the course in which DuMond enrolls. And moreover, if the sociology department has and holds communication to its collective bosom, DuMond won't enroll at all, since he wants a degree in sociology about as much as he wants chocolate mousse in his Tanqueray and Schweppes.

Not only that, but the whole reason behind this book in the first place is to show how Humanity discovered The Meaning of Life, as well as to reveal what that Meaning is. Now, in all honesty, I have to tell you that I don't believe in The Meaning of Life at all, and I never have. The Meaning of Life is a distinctly human concern, and, as far as I know, nobody else in the Galaxy or even our neighbor galaxies has ever thought that Life ought to have a Meaning.

But humans do, and, as I said right at the beginning of this book, Huey and I have become friends over the last 2000 years, and I promised I'd jot down my own objective, outside views on how the Meaning of Life got discovered. So here's this book.

Well, when the communication department and the sociology department decided they didn't want to get together, that was a lesson in The Meaning of Life, although I must say no one was ready to understand it in any deep way that early on. Still I have to show you what happened, because it will be important later.

Take notes, there will be a quiz later. Pencils up!

Chapter 4: The Chair

One of the main elements that made Dean Kurland's plan attractive was that the chair of the Communication Department was himself a sociologist. In fact, he had a degree from the Number One Ranked Sociology Department in the United States. So he was pretty ambivalent about getting married to the sociology department.

On the one hand, while he agreed with the dean about where the two disciplines ranked in the global scheme of University Affairs, he actually had very little to do professionally with communication or sociology, publishing his own research mainly in literary circles. He could be happy in Communication, where he was Chair and held power, so he could control his own life pretty well. Of course, if the department were to be closed, he could be Out Of Work, a catastrophe for a person who, like the chair, had no employable skills whatever.

On the other hand, if he became a Full Professor in the sociology department, he could pretty much retire into his faculty office, teach a few hours a week, and collect a decent paycheck until he either died or became too senile to find his way to work. (In fact, he knew at least two professors back at the Number One Department of Sociology that continued to work even *after* they were senile.) What's more, such a big department was much less likely to be shut down if the Budget Crisis became any worse. Either way, the proposed betrothal would have little effect on his scientific work.

Truth be told, the Chair's "scientific work" pretty much had nothing to do with science at all. Yet he was, by the standards of the communication field, a Really Big Deal. He had achieved this level of preeminence by writing acerbic essays which poked ridicule at those who believed human behavior could be expressed in terms either scientific or mathematical, and he was Really Good at it.

The Chair was among those who believed very deeply in the Meaning of Life. He believed that the Meaning of Life lay deeper than the superficial levels that could be touched by science, and, indeed, believed that scientific scrutiny of human life demeaned and lessened The Meaning of Life. In this he resembled some of Huey's earliest ancestors, such as Socrates and Plato and Confucius.

The Chair believed he had come to accept this view as a result of a lifetime of reasoning based on evidence, but, in fact, his convictions had little to do with any study on his part. They were actually the result of his association with mainly scholars from the Platonic tradition, many of whom accumulated in the social sciences, sociology and rhetoric, the cousin of communication. Whatever the reasons behind the Chair's beliefs, the likelihood that the Communication Chair could earn the respect of Dean Kurland, the neuroscientist, on the basis of his scholarly work was pretty slim.

In spite of these views, the chair was First Class in his job as chair. He knew his faculty well, and he did not let his personal ideology interfere with the success of the department. His decision about mating with the sociologists would rest on his assessment of how much his faculty loved the sociologists and what kind of dowry the Dean might cough up, and not on his own feelings.

After the Incident at Rainbow Bridge, he had 5 faculty left (beside himself). Two were native Buffalonians, and wouldn't leave in either case. One was married to a tenured Associate Professor in the Chemistry department, and certainly wouldn't leave if her husband remained. (They seemed to be getting on well, so the chair assumed they'd stay No Matter What.) The fourth was an outstanding metaphysician whose work he could not comprehend himself, but he knew the credentials of the experts who said he was a *great* metaphysician, so he assumed he was. But, like many metaphysicians, the chair was sure he not only wouldn't care if he became a sociologist, but probably wouldn't notice.

So, for these four plus himself, the marriage was a wash. No one would really care if they mated with the sociologists or not, or, if they did care, they wouldn't do anything about it. And, of course, the extra stability would pretty much ensure that the department wouldn't be eliminated, and, most dreadful of all possibilities, should the department be eliminated, everyone -

- even the chair himself, could be (Yikes!) *fired*, tenure or no.

That left only one more professor to consider, Lu Wi.

Now, you have to understand that the Chair was pretty much against the scientific study of human communication, and had built his reputation attacking those who claimed humanity could be studied scientifically.

But the Chair was, after all, the Chair, and in that role he acknowledged -- even took pride in -- the fact that most Communication Researchers agreed Lu Wi was one of the foremost rookie Communication Scientists in the world. (If she were playing for the Mighty Buffalo Bills, she would definitely have been a #1 First Round Draft Choice.)

To be sure, Lu Wi had a number of strikes against her, what with her being Asian and Female and Mathematical and Breathtakingly Beautiful (the chair bit the heel of his hand as her image crossed his mind) all at once. (Being a woman in the university is pretty tough, but to be a beautiful woman is pretty near suicide.)

Strikes or no, Lu Wi could move if she was pissed, and the Chair knew it. If he even dreamed of keeping her on the staff for a few more years, she'd have to be happy, and so the Chair decided that Lu Wi would be the one who decided whether or not to mate with the sociologists.

Chapter 5: Lu Wi

If ever there was anyone well qualified to be the Mother of Collective Consciousness, Lu Wi was it. Born in Tapei, Taiwan, Republic of China to a family of the loftiest station in the Koumintang, she graduated with highest honors from National Cheng-chi University with specializations in biology and mathematics.

Lu Wi could never have become the great scientist she ultimately became in Old China, for two good reasons. First, and most obvious, women in Old China would never have dreamt of advanced study, nor would they have been afforded it if, by some freak event, they so desired. But there was a less obvious reason: Lu Wi would have been Much Too Important to become a mere scientist.

Lu Wi's Honorable Ancestors had been at the very pinnacle of social and political power, and her blood was definitely of a purplish tinge. Had China remained as it was, Lu Wi might well have been required to turn away from science toward a life of utter uselessness, which was the least that could be expected of a Queen.

But change comes, even to Yu (quiet), Hia (great) Sciam (splendid), Cheu (perfect), Han (the Milky Way), Ta-Min (great brilliance), Ciumhoa (to be at the center), and China, as that great nation has from time to time called itself. In fact, shortly after the Tartars were driven from China, the emperor Humvus, as he was called at the time, decreed that henceforth no one of royal blood should ever again rule in China, so Lu Wi would be pretty much out on that count alone.

On October 1, 1949, Mao Zedong (A.K.A Mao Tse-tung at the time) drove Lu Wi's family (A.K.A Lui, A.K.A. Hui) and two million of their friends and supporters from the mainland of China to the Island of Formosa (A.K.A. Taiwan, A.K.A. The Garden Island), where they formed the Republic of China (A.K.A. Chung-hua Min-kuo).

Over the next few years, Mao was able to find several million more of Lu Wi's friends and family and return them to the Great Chi'i from which we all sprang. But, only moments later, with the millions of Honorable Ancestors still intact in their graves, the Wheel of Change was about to roll once again. (By the time the Wheel rolled, about 50 years had passed, but on Galaxy Central time, half a century is hard to notice.) Before the Millennium (Western time) the ROC and the People's Republic (A.K.A. Mainland China, A.K.A. Red China) were once again, however unofficially, considering merger. Within the last few years, Taiwanese businessmen had been allowed to set up factories on the Mainland, so that, more often than you might imagine, *Made In China* meant *Made in China by a Taiwanese Business.* Perhaps even more important, in the last few months, some of these very rich Taiwanese businessmen had been allowed to bring choice Mainland Maidens back to Taiwan as Brides.

Still, you can imagine that the 20 million citizens of Taiwan were of two minds on the prospect of reuniting with their 1.13 billion friends and relatives on the mainland. Liberated from the weighty restrictions of a five Millennium history of stability and homogeneity, and thrust into the mainstream of Western Capitalism, the island-based Taiwanese exploded into Prosperity.

To be sure, Red China had moved a long way toward Capitalism since the demise of Mao Zedong, and, at most, could be considered a bright pink, or perhaps fuchsia. And she expressed a strong interest in moving the rest of the way toward the 20th century as the world planned to turn the corner into the 21st. There was a mutual hope that the wealthy, savvy, Hyper Modern Taiwanese could take a leading role in the economic development of the Mainland.

On the other hand, no matter how clever or well financed they might be, many felt that the idea that 20 million people could revolutionize over a billion people in a 5000 year old culture was about as realistic as a flea on an elephant's back with a rape in mind.

Nonetheless, the industrious Taiwanese prepared for the transition. And, for as long as anyone in China could remember (which was quite a way back, you can bet) preparation meant education, and plenty of it. So Lu Wi left Taiwan for John Hopkins. Three years later, Lu Wi took her Doctorate in Communication at Hopkins, with a specialization in Convergence Theory, and by Fall was a brand new Assistant Professor of Communication at the University of Buffalo.

Convergence Theory was a theory about how people and cultures changed when they communicated with each other. It was used for the most part to understand the kinds of things that happened to immigrants' heads when they moved to a new and foreign culture. And, as you might recall, Taiwan and Mainland China were about to merge into One Country again. Unless something very sophisticated was done, Convergence Theory predicted that the 20 million Taiwanese would converge on the Billion Plus mainlanders in the blink of an eye, leaving nothing of their advanced economic standing worth speaking of.

And Convergence Theory wasn't just another soft-cover self-help laundry list of recipes for successful communication. It was a deeply *mathematical* theory, and Lu Wi liked mathematics better than Kilmer liked trees. For a stranger in a strange land like herself, a mathematical theory to illuminate her own angst was too much to resist.

Even better, Convergence theory was deeply related to another theory, even more abstract and mathematical, called Galileo Theory, which described all thought processes, both individual and collective, with gorgeous, simply gorgeous equations. Perceptions and concepts were damped harmonic oscillators vibrating in a high-dimensional Riemann space, and the tensors that described their non-euclidean eigenfunctions made Lu Wi warm in secret places.

Could things be even more appropriate? You bet they could, since the Galileo theory had an applied side, and the most common application of Galileo Theory was in manipulating people's attitudes and beliefs on a Really Large Scale. (At Hopkins they spent a Bundle of Money each year designing Galileo strategies to promote family planning throughout the developing world, and most everyone agreed the Galileo strategies were more effective than anything anyone else had yet figured out.)

Twenty Million divided by 1.13 Billion is still less than 2%, which was what percentage of the Mainland Chinese the Taiwanese made up. But a technology as potent as the Galileo might help even the odds, so there were, at any given moment, a half dozen or more Taiwanese in the US studying Galileos. They were studying real hard, too, since there were about that many Mainlanders doing exactly the same thing.

With her Hopkins degree, her immense skill and her Totally Politically Correct Asian Femaleness, Lu Wi could have gone pretty much wherever she wanted, but there was only one place she ever wanted to go -- Buffalo.

Now, people from the late 20th century would have thought that too farfetched even for light fiction, but those people would have been wrong. For reasons even I don't know, 20th Century Americans developed an exaggerated distaste for winter along with an even more exaggerated belief in the severity of *Buffalo's* winters. As I've said earlier, this reputation had begun to decline by the 1990's, partly because the Mighty Buffalo Bills rolling across the American Football Conference brought a lot of favorable attention to the Queen City -- they even televised nationally games played in Buffalo when it was pretty obviously a (Yikes!) Really Nice Day.

But, strange to say, Buffalo never developed a bad reputation outside the United States. People in Taipei, for example, or Seoul, did not refer to Buffalo as the Armpit of the East, nor did they believe, as many Americans still did in the 1990's, that Pittsburgh was a dirty industrial city. Unhampered by decades old prejudices, foreigners were able to form more accurate opinions of America than Americans.

(Speaking of Pittsburgh, three days after Lu Wi gave Dewey DuMond a copy of ROVER, a computer program that led, one might say, directly to the Voice of New Humanity, and which I will tell you about in due time, the Mighty Buffalo Bills beat the red-hot Pittsburgh Stealers 28-20 at Orchard Park, which was where the Mighty Bills actually played home games. The game was televised nationwide, and, as anyone could plainly see, it was a Very Nice Day in Orchard Park.)

Among the offers of employment Lu Wi rejected before accepting the Buffalo bid was one from the University of Wisconsin at Madison, Wisconsin, a city that Life Magazine once considered the Best City to Live In in the Whole United States, Bar None. Nestled among Lakes Mendota, Menona and Wingra, and blessed with the lovely University of Wisconsin campus, the State Capital complete with its classic imitation of the Capital in Washington Dead Center Downtown, Madison had a lot to offer.

Among the things Madison had to offer was Deep Historical Significance, since the University of Wisconsin at Madison was, if not the birthplace, at least the Place of Impregnation of the Galileo Theory. Another was Cold. Not just cold, like Buffalo, whose reputation for hard winters made it into the Armpit of the East for most Americans. Buffalo was cold for sure. But

Madison was Cold with a capital "C". Boldface, even.

How cold was it? Madison, Wisconsin was so cold, that often in January or February the thermometer would spend a week or even two below zero, seldom or never reaching that magic mark even during the warmest(!) part of the day. (In Buffalo, to give you a fair standard of comparison, it was not unusual for an entire winter to go by without the temperature once falling as low as zero.) During her brief sojourn in Madison for her interview, Lu Wi would personally see a thermometer read -33. (In Buffalo, to give you another fair comparison, the year Lu Wi enrolled at Johns Hopkins, the coldest day of the entire year -- February 25 -- was +2.)

Thus it was that The Most Ideal City To Live In in the Entire United States Bar None compared to the City of Good Neighbors, the Queen City of the Great Lakes, the great and fearful winter wonderland of the Northeast, the Armpit of the East, Buffalo, New York. How *about* that, Sports Fans!

Lu Wi would have gone to Buffalo even if it had been the Armpit it was believed to be, because the communication department at Buffalo was also the location of the two foremost proponents of Galileo Theory in the world. (In spite of the seminal role Wisconsin had played in the development of Galileo Theory, no serious student of Galileo Theory remained at that worthy institution.)

No matter how lovely others might think Niagara Falls, the Niagara River, Lakes Erie and Ontario, Cataraugus and Ellicott Creeks, the Boston Hills, the glorious autumn leaves and a hundred other beauties of the Queen City of the Great Lakes, all these paled into insignificance beside the beauty of the Galileo Equations in Lu Wi's mind. And Buffalo was the Home Office, the Factory Outlet Store for Galileos, and that's where she wanted to be.

No sooner had she arrived, however, than Lu Wi herself become the foremost exponent of Galileo Theory at the University of Buffalo. Alas, this was not due to a sudden increase in her own skills. Lu Wi's elevation was more abruptly and directly the result of the fact that the two stalwarts who previously commanded this lofty position were, at that exact moment, spinning dizzyingly from shore to shore of the Whirlpool Rapids at the base of Niagara Falls.

And so it was that, before she ever set foot inside a Buffalo classroom -- before, indeed, she had unpacked her books in her new office, Lu Wi sat in Dean Kurland's immense office, the future of the Communication Department hanging heavy in her hands.

Chapter 6: Lu Wi and Curly

For those of you not intimately familiar with the bowels of the academic community, it's helpful to know that the Difference in Status between the Dean of a Major Faculty in a Major Public Research University and a rookie assistant professor is about the same as the difference between a Bishop and a nun, so Lu Wi would have had every reason for feeling intimidated. And, in full fairness to Dean Kurland, it must be said that it would have been an extraordinary person of either gender who would not be slightly intoxicated by the huge social power he wielded over this luscious babe. Remember as well that the Dean had been under a severe strain for a long time, was surrounded by sycophants and mortal enemies, and thus did not have a good sense of himself and how he was behaving.

Perhaps we can understand, if not condone, the subtle ways he made eye contact with Lu Wi; the way he postured his body toward her, the way he rose from behind his desk to sit, first in the overstuffed chair across the coffee table from Lu Wi, then moved again to sit next to her on the leather couch, all the while droning seductively about the advantages to be accrued by all if the Sociology Department were to "absorb" the communication department. The Dean's words were made all the more convincing by the fact that he deeply believed them himself.

Lu Wi smelled rape from the first word. She wasn't half as intimidated as the Dean was intoxicated, because her family back in the ROC had the power to order Deans like Curly buried in open pits without a warrant. Nor did she believe that the Dean would rape her, but it was as plain as warts on a princess that the Dean was planning to rape the Communication Department, and maybe the sociologists, too.

Lu Wi was right about the merger, but she was wrong about the Dean. By now he was dazed and confused, and interpreted every inscrutable gesture, every movement Lu Wi made as an invitation for his further advances. He squeezed still closer.

Just how crazed by lust the Dean was is obvious, since he was already in court on Failure to Educate complaints, another faculty member was up on sexual harassment charges and two more were being investigated, and the bodies of Lu Wi's colleagues and students were still wet with the water of the mighty Niagara River. Nonetheless, without any volition on his part, his hands reached out and grabbed Lu Wi's left arm just above the elbow, and he started to pull her to him. He said a number of things about her beauty and his need and the rightness of what he hoped was about to happen, although, to his credit, he never said anything about job benefits or future favors as a reward for her cooperation.

Dean Kurland need not have worried about a lawsuit from Lu Wi. Lu Wi was a true professional who would never air her dirty linen in public. Whatever happened in the university stayed in the university as far as she was concerned. Lu Wi was part of the Old Boy Network, and she wouldn't compromise her principles. So she did something else entirely.

Lu Wi's right arm cocked, her hand balled into a fist, and, quicker than you could say "neurotransmitter", Lu Wi had decked the Dean.

Chapter 7: Dewey

D. W. "Dewey" DuMond walked aimlessly along Manhattan Beach in Los Angeles, A.K.A. LA, the City of the Angels, "La La Land" and a long list of other names. He was supposed to be at the console of his DEC workstation in the marketing department of Hughes Aircraft at that very moment, helping the staff figure out how to use the new Galileo System software they had just installed, but Dewey found he couldn't pay attention.

When he first interviewed at Hughes, Dewey had visions of cutting edge computing in top secret artificial intelligence projects, but instead found himself in the Marketing Department about to install marketing research software. When the Galileo software first ran, it popped up a menu that said, in a very colorful and attractive visual screen, to be sure, "boring, boring, boring..." Dewey took a quick glance at the menu of items, which promised such thrilling functions as "Make a Questionnaire," "Make Tables", "Run CATPAC" (whatever that was), "Make a screen plot," and, -- be still, my beating heart -- "count votes." There were a few other options, but they all seemed equally boring. A real snoozer, Galileo. Dewey headed for the beach.

Conceived on February 8, 1969 in London, England, and born two months early on September 4 of that year in the City of Angels,

Dewey and his parents had moved to Amherst, New York when he was two years old. There he had played Defensive End for the Buffalo Bulls, the Division III football team of the University at Buffalo, while working toward his degree in Computer Science, granted with great honors just three months before his 21st birthday.

Dewey had always been an enterprising lad. He played keyboards in various rock and jazz bands around the Queen City -- he once sat in with Blue Lou at the Tralfalmador Cafe -- and had operated a small computer games business since his junior year at Buffalo. Dewey didn't deal with spare time well, and wasn't much of a fan of beaches either, so his stroll along the Beach was a pretty exotic experience for him.

DuMond's fiancée, a Piano Performance graduate student at UCLA, had only recently flown into a bridge in Washington, D.C. on an airliner commanded by two pilots from the South who hadn't spent enough time in the Queen City of the Great Lakes to develop respect for Snow on the Wings. One passenger whose identity I will protect turned to his seat mate as the wings filled with snow and joked "At least we're not going to Buffalo!" Moments later the snow covered DC-9 tried its mightiest to mate with the frozen bridge.

(At 12:30 AM, November 5th, 1992, when President Elect William Clinton made his acceptance speech from the steps of the Capital in Little Rock, Arkansas, marking the beginning of the period when Huey first rolled across the Green Hills of Earth, it was precisely 14 degrees colder in that bastion of the Deep South than it was in Buffalo, the Queen City of the Great Lakes. But it was colder than both those places in Madison, you can bet.)

The last few months in Los Angeles had lost some magic after the plane went to its watery grave, his job at Hughes didn't allow much freedom to explore the kinds of computing he found interesting, and, like many a bright young man and woman eager to depart the Armpit of the East, after a few years away Dewey began to miss the Queen City.

What's more, he was just in the early stages of a ricochet romance with the keyboard. Not the keyboard of his hot DEC workstation, or even the Fender Rhodes and Rolands he'd played so many times in dimly lit places in Buffalo, but the brand new Yamaha grand he'd bought with the first fruits of his fat salary at Hughes. Intoxicated by his new lover, Dewey couldn't listen to another note of jazz, blues, rock, or any other kind of electric music. Dewey had discovered Mozart, Bach, Beethoven, Chopin, and the boys, and he was hooked.

Dazed and confused as he was, Dewey stepped on a football lying on the sand and stumbled to his knees next to an unemployed aircraft worker from Lancaster, NY, who had come to California to avoid exactly the fate that had befallen him shortly after he arrived. After some smiles and apologies, the two struck up a conversation, tossed around the football, then moved on to a sequence of bars where they consumed mass quantities of Anchor Steam Beer and reminisced about the City of Good Neighbors.

The next day, still dazed but no longer confused, Dewey leaped, eyes open, into the exact fate his new friend was struggling to escape, phoned his Boss at Hughes and told him to send his last checks to him care of General Delivery in Amherst, NY, home of the University at Buffalo, A.K.A. The State University of New York at Buffalo.

As soon as he arrived, Dewey rented a small apartment in Getzville, just north of Amherst, and submitted his application to the Music Department. Piano Performance Program, of the University at Buffalo. There was, however, a slight snag Dewey had not anticipated: he was not admitted. The recession that sent Dewey's newest California friend into unemployment had not left the University at Buffalo unscathed, and the Piano Performance program had become only one of the long string of victims of trickle down economics. A *magna cum laude* degree in Computer Science wasn't enough to get Dewey one of the very few slots available in the Piano Performance program.

And so it was, unemployed and with nothing to do but tend to his small computer software hobby/business, that Dewey enrolled in a course in the Communication Department through the Millard Fillmore Adult College. It was called

Com 571: Seminar in Neural Networks and Cognitive Processes.

The course description said it would explore questions of neural networks, pattern recognition, storage and retrieval, consciousness and culture. It would relate these abstruse topics to Galileo Theory, which struck a familiar chord in Dewey's memories from Hughes.

According to the Catalog, it would be taught by a new Assistant Professor named Lu Wi.

Chapter 8: Larry

Angelo Lawrence Black was born in Millard Fillmore Hospital in The City of Good Neighbors, the Queen City of the Great Lakes, August 15, 1924. Angelo Lawrence's Mama called him Angelo, but his friends called him "Angel", which he didn't like, so he wrote his name, from the first day of high school until his death as a very old man, " A. Lawrence Black." In his own private mind, he thought of himself as Larry.

When he was eleven years old, the big old radio in his Mama's house stopped dead in the middle of a Fireside Chat, and for the next two days Larry poked around in it until he found a small cylinder encircled by brown, orange, yellow and silver stripes that looked a bit cooked. He cut it out with Mama's fingernail clipper, took it to a store that said something like "Radio Electronics Warehouse" on Elm street, and after laying out 4 cents, Larry wound a shiny new cylinder just like the old burned one into the radio.

When the Benny Goodman Trio swung out of the big old speaker, Mama and was all the more convinced that he was a Really Talented Kid, and from that time on, encouraged Larry to study scientific stuff.

On August 14, 1942, he and three of his friends spotted a black 1937 Buick Special parked at the side of Jefferson Street with the doors unlocked, and those three buddies inquired as to whether Larry was bright enough to make that car run without keys. He was, and before he was completely sure of what was happening, Larry was lying face down in the middle of the street in front of the Sattler's Department Store, 998 Broadway, with red lights flashing in his eyes, police radios crackling in his ears, and Buffalo's Finest asking, real loud, what he was doing in somebody else's car.

The following morning, just after the dawning of Larry's 18th year on the green hills of earth, he and two more Finest stood at the doorstep of his Mama's house, where the officers explained to Mama that Larry was either about to go to the Erie County Correctional Facility in Alden, NY, or to Germany. Larry chose Germany, and, four weeks later, was in Kentucky, on his way to Louisiana.

Larry volunteered for the Army Air Corps, but they weren't accepting any Negroes from the City of Good Neighbors at that time, thank you, and the sergeant suggested that the Tank Corps was the toughest, friendliest, most patriotic and all round congenial places for a bright young man like Larry to find his fortune. Larry had never driven a car before, not even the Buick that took him to Kentucky via Sattlers, and the idea of driving a big old tank seemed like a fine, fine experience. Quick like a bunny, Larry was a private in the 461st Tank Corps at the side of a Really Warm Bayou in Louisiana.

Larry was a very bright young man, and he knew that not everyone in the City of Good Neighbors was equally neighborly. But, even so, nothing in the Queen City had prepared him for Louisiana.

Larry's first weekend pass took him into town, where he wandered into a grocery store on the White side of town. Two Big, White, Friendly MP's brought him back to the barracks, where they turned him over to two Big, Black, Not Friendly MP's who taught him The Meaning of Life for about 15 minutes.

The bruises from his lesson about The Meaning of Life had faded into a dim memory when Larry arrived in England, where the local population had not yet learned how to discriminate properly against Negroes. The U.S. Army, however, had prepared for this eventuality, and explained repeatedly to the friendly British that the Negro Soldier had to be carefully watched, especially where white women were concerned.

They were thoughtful enough to explain as well that there was no need for excessive gratitude toward these swarthy soldiers, since they were only here to deliver the tanks to the white soldiers who, blessed with superior fighting reflexes and deeper moral values, would push the Hun back into the Black Forest quicker than you could say "Jack Robinson."

Larry soon found himself in France, where the 461st kicked open door after door in Patton's relentless quest to close the Bulge. Just before the final success, Larry's tank was hit by an anti-tank gun his unit had been assured wasn't there, and he woke up under a snowdrift at the side of a French road with a piece of shrapnel through his helmet and part way into his head. A 17-year-old white boy from New Orleans rolled Larry off the edge of the road into a ditch out of the line of fire just as a German 50 caliber sent that fine young Southern boy a few steps lower on the food chain.

When he woke up, the sounds of battle had dimmed to a dull roar. Hidden as he was in the safety of the snow, he'd been left behind by his embattled unit as it rolled relentlessly toward Germany.

Larry climbed unsteadily to his feet and considered his plight: harassed as they were, the tanks could still make an easy 7 or 8 MPH along the little road, and Larry was too wobbly to make anything like that pace. If he stayed where he was, he'd be picked up soon enough by another unit, but, in these parts, the odds weren't too much in favor of that unit being American.

As he considered his plight, he saw a small figure moving toward him from a nearby farmhouse. There was something odd about the way it moved, but, as it grew closer, Larry's fuzzy brain realized it was a small boy on a bicycle. The boy jumped off the bicycle and walked it the last three or four feet to Larry, shouting over and over,

"La Bicyclette, La Bicyclette!"

He pushed the vehicle into Larry's unsteady hands and continued saying "La Bicyclette" while he pointed down the road toward Larry's vanishing unit.

Larry woke up in a field hospital not too far from Rouen as a Brigadier General walked among the many beds. He stopped to speak to each wounded soldier, to pass some encouragement, and to tell them all how much the Great Experiment of Washington and Jefferson depended on their sacrifice, until he stopped in front of Larry.

"What's the matter, Boy," said the BG. "Got the Clap?"

This was a Pretty Tense Moment, as you can imagine, until a Good Old Boy from a town outside Baton Rouge so small it had no name, in a body cast from his neck to his toes, said in a loud clear voice,

"General, if he's got it, he got it from yo Mama!"

That white boy was back in the United States before the month was out, but Larry recovered quickly and, as the months sped by, found himself third tank in a column of tanks before a steel gate in Germany. The first tank smashed down the gate and stopped. There was a lot of confusion, and Larry watched his fellow soldiers in the first two tanks climb, dazed and confused, out of their own steel machines. He climbed out of his own tank after them, walked toward the gate and saw a sign that said "Buchenwald", and beneath that, in the middle of the gate, a German phrase he couldn't read which he learned later said something like "Every Man For Himself."

Beyond the gate was a scene Larry never completely absorbed, although he saw it in his dreams as long as he lived.

Larry never knew that the Jews and Gypsies and Other Minor Races in the camp would forever see his black visage in their sleep, or remember Black Angels as the Liberators of Buchenwald. But, in the weeks that followed, he knew that he had learned yet another meaning of the word "racism."

After the war, Larry landed a job as a janitor at Buffalo Forge deep in the bowels of the City of Good Neighbors, where he met a young veteran who had also served under General George. His new friend was a machinist, and, in his spare time, a Six Day Bike Racer.

The two traded stories about Patton and tanks and snow and French Wine, but Larry never mentioned Buchenwald, which had taught him not only the meaning of racism but also the meaning of "unspeakable."

Larry's inability to speak about Buchenwald wasn't the only emotional souvenir he brought back from Europe. He also carried home a deep attachment to bicycles. Before he landed the job at Buffalo Forge, Larry had already bought a used Shelby with some of his mustering out pay, then traded that for a small profit and bought a Roadmaster. He was on his fifth bicycle, a huge, indestructible Schwinn not unlike the tank that carried him across France deep into Germany, when the Six Day Bike Racer showed him the Peugot he raced.

This little wisp of a bicycle knocked Larry's socks off. That weekend Larry pedaled desperately through the Queen City, but nowhere was there anything like the spidery Peugeot to be found. On Monday he asked his friend to help him get one, and, with all the connections of a Six Day Bike Racer, it took Larry seven months to score a prewar Peugeot.

While he waited for the Peugeot, Larry bought and sold more than a dozen used bicycles out of his Mama's house on Meech Avenue near

Canisius College. He also learned as much as he could about machinery at Buffalo Forge, and, urged on by his Mama, began a habit that would last his entire lifetime: he enrolled for an adult education course at Hutchinson Central Technical High School. Larry would take one course every Fall and one more every Spring for the rest of his very long life.

Chapter 9: SPOT

Dewey admitted to a slight curiosity about what a "Galileo" might be, since integrating the new Galileo Software into Hughes Aircraft's computing system was the assignment that was on his plate the very day he punked out of that worthy firm. Truth be told, he had no idea what a Galileo might be, other than a long-dead astronomer.

Moreover, (more truth), as a Computer Scientist and Engineer, his opinion of social science was even lower than Dean Kurland's, and his first encounter with the Galileo menu had been, uh, unstimulating.

He was, however, very interested in artificial neural networks. A friend of his in the computer games business had slipped him an outlaw copy of an artificial neural network called "SPOT," which, Dewey thought, had a lot of promise.

SPOT worked like this:

Think of a theatre marquee with plenty of lightbulbs. More appropriately, you might think of the Electronic Scoreboard at Bills' Stadium in Orchard Park, home of the Buffalo Bills. (Dewey liked to think of neurons as lightbulbs.) Now you can make that marquee or scoreboard represent just about any pattern you can think of simply by turning some of those bulb-nuerons on and leaving the rest off.

(You've seen the scoreboard at Bill's Stadium display the word "Touchdown!", show explosions, fireworks, the American flag, replays of key plays, on Monday Night Football. Even if you haven't, you know what I mean. If you're old enough to read this book yourself, you've seen a theatre marquee somewhere.)

And so, if you will, pretend we've turned on enough "bulberons" to spell out

"How are you, SPOT?"

Nothing to it.

Now imagine a second marquee, and imagine someone has connected up the lightbulbs in the first marquee to the lightbulbs in the second one so that, whenever you turn on the ones that say "How are you, SPOT?" in the first marquee, they in turn light up some other ones on the second marquee so that *they* spell

"Not too bad, Thanks."

You've just made a very primitive Artificial Neural Network. Can you say "Artificial Neural Network," Boys and Girls?

From here to a really powerful, (and really useful) neural network is pretty straightforward. (Straightforward but tedious, as the great Richard A. Holmes Jr., whose Memorial

Computing Laboratory plays such a large role in this story, used to say.)

There are four steps:

Step 1: Make more bulbs, make them smaller, and put them closer together. (This means you can make a more detailed picture or pattern)

Step 2: Make the bulbs adjustable to be dimmer and brighter, instead of just "on" or "off". (Such bulbs have continuous or "analog" values, which you have to know so you'll understand later why Lu Wi and Dewey go to so much expense to get an analog chip made for them.)

Step 3: Put another marquee between the first two, so you now have and input marquee (input layer), and output marquee (output layer) and a middle or "hidden" marquee (hidden layer). Our more powerful artificial neural network is going to use this hidden layer as a switching bank to control the connections between the input bulbs and the output bulbs.

Step 4: Figure out some way to rewire the connections among the layers whenever the network outputs the wrong thing. (Actually you won't have to do that, because some Really Smart People have already done that for you.)

Now you've got a real nice toy on your hands, as, indeed, SPOT was, for all intents and purposes, meant as a toy, and sold as a toy, for the price of a toy ($19.95, including a free T-shirt with a picture of SPOT on the front and the message "My computer is smarter than your dog" on the back.)

Can you say "supervised three-layer analog feed-forward back-propagation artificial neural network," Boys and Girls?

As I said, SPOT was made as a sort of educational toy for learning about neural networks, and it was able to learn to hold a conversation with you. You would give it a list of questions and answers, like

Q: How are you, SPOT?

A: I'm fine, thank you.

Q: Where do you live, SPOT?

A: On your hard drive, Chemical Brain.

And SPOT, slowly but surely, would learn the right answers for the right questions. But SPOT didn't learn immediately, like a regular computer program. It took some time to rewire its brain, and this was done only a bit at a time, so SPOT would seem to be learning just like a real, Chemical Brain person, getting closer and closer to the right answer until it finally got it.

And, once it got it, it would give the right answer *even if you didn't get the question exactly right.* So you could ask it

"How are you, SPIT?"

and it would say, sure as shootin',

"I'm fine, thank you."

In fact, you could say

"How you doin, Buddy?"

and SPOT would give the right answer, or at least one pretty close. (It might say something like, "A'm well, phanc you.", but you'd know what it meant.)

Dewey used up all the demonstration files that came with SPOT, then wrote a few of his own. After a while, he figured out how to get SPOT to call offensive plays.

As a former Defensive End for the Buffalo Bulls, Dewey was, of course, interested in football, and remained a steadfast Bills fan even after leaving the Queen City for California, home of the Rams, the Forty Niners, The Raiders and the Chargers.

(At that time, California, the largest state in the U.S., had four National Football League teams, while New York, the second largest state, had only one, the Buffalo Bills, since the Jets and Giants, although still wearing the New York name, actually played all their home games in New Jersey. You'll also want to remember that the Bills, a great NFL team who had the most profound effect on Huey's ultimate values, should not be confused with the Bulls, the University of Buffalo's struggling collegiate team.)

But not only was Dewey a steadfast fan, he was, as a Former Defensive End, deeply interested in guessing just what play the offensive team would run, and in understanding what clues might give their plans away. The long suit of a Defensive End is speed and quickness, since what he has to do depends entirely on what the offensive team does. A Defensive End who can guess a split second earlier what play is going to develop has a decisive advantage.

So, instead of giving SPOT some questions like "Who's buried in Grant's tomb?" and teaching SPOT to answer something like "Is this a trick question?", Dewey would give SPOT information about the score, what quarter it was, what the team's standing was, what down it was, how many yards to first down, which key defensive and offensive players were injured, and so on. And he would ask SPOT to guess the play the offensive team would call in response to these factors.

And, as for the correct answers, (which he wanted SPOT to be able to provide) he trained SPOT with the actual plays called in every NFL game that he could find on the national computer network -- which was what we technically call Really a Lot of Games.

SPOT cranked away day and night for a Really Long Time, and, finally, said it was ready to discuss plays with Dewey. To Dewey's amazement, SPOT turned out to be a pretty decent quarterback -- as long is it didn't have to actually throw a pass or anything, but only had to call plays. Not Jim Kelly, mind you, the great quarterback of the mighty Buffalo Bills, but good enough, good enough.

What excited Dewey more than SPOT's skill as a play caller was the way it worked. A neural network worked completely differently from a conventional computer program.

A conventional "serial" program was entirely made by a programmer. Everything a conventional program could do was written in by the programmer, so there were never any surprises in what it could or would do (mistakes, yes; blunders, of course! -- but never, ever a surprise.) And, conventional programs were exact and unforgiving. Give a conventional program an input and it gave you a precise output, pronto. But spell the input wrong, and it tells you something insulting, like

>bad command or file name.

Finally, regular serial computer programs are great at math, and make calculations with lightning speed. Ask a regular computer program the square root of 69 and, lickety split, it tells you 13.11992000 as fast as you can look at it.

But neural networks work differently. First, they have to learn whatever it is you want them to do by studying examples you give them. You may not be aware of what they have read and learned, and so they can behave in ways that surprise even the programmer.

Secondly, they're not very precise, and can get the drift of what you want even if you misspell it or get it almost but not quite right. And last but not least, they're not very good at math. If you ask a neural network for the square root of 69, it tells you "8 something."

They work a lot like people.

So Dewey was intrigued by the Neural Network course, even though it was offered by the Communication Department and not Computer Science. Actually, Dewey didn't think badly of Communication because it was a social science. He didn't even know it was a social science because he had no idea what Communication was at all.

Chapter 10: Policy on Class Attendance

At the graduate level, very few Professors have a mandatory class attendance policy. You are full grown adults, and you have to decide for yourself how your time is best spent. Some classes are too easy for you, and it's a waste of your time to go to them. Others are beyond your present level, so you couldn't understand them anyway. Still others are just what you need, and you ought to attend.

I've recorded what happened in some of Lu Wi's classes, but your attendance is optional. Like, for example, in the next chapter I describe

Lu Wi's first class. Certain things happen in that class, to wit:

o We find out that Dewey is attracted to Lu Wi Big Time,

o Dewey's classmates are introduced. They are A. Lawrence Black, a 67 year old Bicycle and Roller Skate shop owner whom you've already met, Richard, his son and partner and Little Richard Imitator, and two auto mechanics/radio personalities from Massachusetts.

o The Galileo System is described at an introductory level (requiring no math). Galileo is a cutting edge software system for measuring and manipulating public opinion.

o The concept of a Neural Network is introduced, and this will be important later.

Now the same thing applies to you and Lu Wi's classes. You can go to them or skip them, depending on your skills and interest. The next chapter, The First Class, is pretty turgid, in my opinion, even if I did write it. Remember, I'm no scientist, rocket or otherwise, and not much of the class was very interesting to me. And you really don't have to know that technical stuff to understand the story I'm telling you here.

On the other hand, if you want to understand, in a technical sense, how a consciousness like Huey is possible, you might want to attend the classes. If not, you can skip them. (You can always get somebody's notes afterward.)

Chapter 11: First Class

Dewey had been away from the University only two years, but even so, the trip from engagement to bereavement, from Hughes Aircraft and $48,500 a year back to Unemployment and UB, had been abrupt. None of this would prove so unsettling to Dewey, however, as the fist sight of Lu Wi.

These shocks to his system, and even more so the aloneness of LA without his fiancee, had led him to be unaware of himself. No one is less aware of himself or herself than a person without friends and associates to see them and report on what they see.

So it isn't too surprising that Dewey hadn't really realized that a lot of the unsettled feelings he had were the result of simple horniness. When he saw Lu Wi, he realized quicker than a Cray II could find the square root of 69 that he was a young man in the peak of his sexual powers who had not touched a woman for half a year.

Now we all know the real source of Dewey's excitement, and it wasn't Lu Wi's intellectual powers, although those were formidable indeed. And, from what little he did grasp about what Lu Wi had said, he thought she would be talking about something like "collective consciousness" or "cognitive space."

Without the juices his glands were pumping out in huge abundance, Dewey would undoubtedly have found this about as interesting as out-of-body experiences and Pyramid Power. Dewey was an engineer, and this sort of nonsense had the smack of Incense, Tie Dye and Mush for Brains.

What's more, Dewey's fellow students were an odd group, to say the least, consisting of only a 68 year old man named A. Lawrence Black who manufactured and sold custom made bicycles, his son, Richard, who looked utterly and completely like Little Richard (Dewey would learn later that he was one of the most accomplished Little Richard Imitators in the US), and a couple of auto mechanics/radio personalities from Boston who were originating out of WBFO, the campus Public Radio Station, while one of them was visiting professor at UB for a semester. While Dewey, truth be told, thought these four were a fascinating quartet of human beings, it was really a stretch to think he might have anything in common with any of them.

Had Lu Wi been ugly, Dewey would have been out the door before you could say "Elvis is alive and working in an A&W Root Beer Stand in Madison, Wisconsin." But, of course, although beauty is in the eye of the beholder, few men

could behold Lu Wi without making some
Adjustments.

Now, after we filter out the effects of
massive testosterone poisoning on Dewey, here's
what Lu Wi had said that Wednesday Night:

First, she introduced the concept of
"object." She used "object" in a very general way,
like the object of a sentence or the object of
attention. It didn't have to be a material object,
because an idea could be an object as long as you
where thinking about it, that is, as long as it was
the object of your attention. (Dewey missed a
good deal of this, because his glands were
making his brain try to remember the words to

> "The object of my affection
> Can change my complexion
> From white to rosy red...")

The second thing Lu Wi said was that
there were no objects in nature, but that what
anyone thought was an object was determined
by his or her own situation, and how other

people (like, society, eh?) taught you to look at things. Like, for example, Dewey's fevered mind thought, some Monk in Tibet sees this teacher as a whole person, but everything in me wants to see two breasts, two legs, some really long, really shiny black hair, and ... oh, my, how embarrassing! He felt guilty objectifying her breasts, but, Great Gosh Almighty, any reasonable jury would decide in a flash he had no choice in the matter. (We won't spend as much time describing how he objectified her legs, but, you get the idea.)

The next thing she said, which made sense to Dewey in spite of his intoxication and his prejudices, was that all these "objects" could be thought of as lying in a big old "space," which Lu Wi called "Galileo Space." Similar things clustered together in that space. So, if you had a bouncy yellow ball, that ball would be found in the "Galileo space" nearby three other objects named "round," "yellow," and "bouncy." In Dewey's Galileo space, Lu Wi would have been found hear the objects "beautiful," "Exciting," "female," and a few others he didn't make explicit.

To illustrate her point, Lu Wi called up a picture on the computer. The class moved closer to the screen. To the left bottom, and, it seemed, sort of toward the front of the picture, he saw some circles, and printed next to each of the circles was a word: SUN, SAND, SURF, PALM TREES, SAN DIEGO. To the right top and toward the back, were circles labelled CITY, GOOD, NEIGHBORS, FRIENDLY, BUFFALO, NIAGARA. And near the top center, closer to Buffalo than San Diego, more circles labelled BIG, EXCITING, FUN, DETROIT.

Even with as little confidence as he had in Social Science, Dewey had no trouble understanding the picture. It meant Buffalo was a city, had neighbors, was good and friendly. (Actually, it meant Buffalo was a friendly place called The City of Good Neighbors, and it was close to Niagara Falls, but Dewey was more than close enough.)

It also meant was that people thought of San Diego as Sun, Sand, Surf, and Palm Trees. Dewey thought this was a great example, very clear.

The little map also meant Detroit was a Big City, which people considered exciting and fun. Dewey had never been in Detroit, so he had even worse prejudices about it than most Americans had about Buffalo. Detroit, A.K.A "The Motor City", A.K.A. "Murder City" had gotten a bad press in the US for a few decades. He didn't know how anyone could think well of Detroit, but, then, he didn't know any better. Later in the semester, though, A. Lawrence Black's son Richard, A.K.A. "Big Dick," A.K.A. "Little Richard" professionally, would remind Dewey that Detroit was A.K.A. "Motown," and the musician in Dewey would be ashamed of his prejudice.

His engineer's mind started to leap ahead. *If someone's opinion about an object began to change, that object would start to move through the space. If somebody started to think Detroit was friendly, for example, the little circle that represented Detroit in the space would have to move toward the "Friendly" circle.* Dewey could see the equations that would describe that movement right away -- they came right out of Freshman Calculus, which every engineering student in the world studied four hours a night. *Neat!*

But his engineer-mind also saw quickly that any really complicated ideas would soon prove to much for this simple three dimensional map, and that a more complete picture would take up too many dimensions to be shown in a simple picture.

"Uh, Professor, uh, Wi", Dewey raised his hand. (He didn't know whether to call her "Professor Wi" or "Professor Lu", but she didn't correct him.)

"What about carrots, oranges and tangerines?" he asked.

"That's a really good question, Mr., uh, Mr. DuMond?" She looked at her class list. Can you explain to the rest of the class what you're asking?"

"Well," Dewey began, " A carrot would be close to "orange", because it's, well, *orange*. And an orange would be close to a tangerine, because they're both fruit. But a carrot wouldn't be too close to a tangerine, because they're quite different."

That caused a bit of a stir in the class, and Dewey was impressed to see the other students seemed to have no problem grasping his question at all. In fact, one of the auto mechanics said right away that that could only be the case if the space were warped or bent, and he drew a picture on a piece of paper, which he then folded over until, eh voila! -- the carrot was close to the orange, the orange was close to the tangerine, and the carrot and the tangerine were pretty far apart.

"Very good!", Lu Wi said. "This picture on the computer is only to help you understand how the meaning of words can be represented mathematically. Complicated ideas can't be drawn in only two or three dimensions, but they can be represented quite exactly in a high-dimensional non-euclidean space with a computer and some equations."

OK, Dewey thought, maybe not *Freshman* Calculus. But he got the idea.

Now, if you're a regular human being and not a University Person, you may be having a hard time understanding how five otherwise normal people could spend three hours talking and arguing about high-dimensional non-euclidean spaces. Don't worry. You ought to be. Truth be told (you heard it here first), most of what gets people excited in the University is, alas, bovine fecal matter (A.K.A. Bullshit). (Great Gosh Almighty, once you get into the University Mode, you can't even *talk* like a real person!)

But, c'mon, now, wait a minute, wait a minute, I know you're easily upset about your Tax Dollars being wasted -- but give me another minute!

There's a reason to waste all this money on the Universities, even though I'm the first to admit that most of the time they can be dumber than a box of rocks. The reason is that *some of what they do is sensational!* And this non-euclidean, high dimensional Galileo stuff is pretty sensational, believe me. You give me a minute and I'll show you.

Larry the Bicycle Man is even more reasonable and sensible than you are, no matter who you are. And he got more than a little nervous during all this technobabble. That's why he was bold enough to ask Lu Wi (whom he respected as an Educated Person):

"Professor Lu," he said, "I believe I can understand that you can actually do this thing. And I think I can even get the gist of how you do it. And, after a while, I can even see how this Galileo space can help you understand the opinions of people. But I've got to say I'm not sure why you want to do this. Just what is this Galileo Space good for?"

Lu Wi stopped for a moment, then began slowly. She herself had two reasons for her interest in the Galileo. One of them was the simple, formal, mathematical beauty of the theory itself. In this she was just like most of the rest of the faculty who thought it was perfectly OK for the taxpayers to support them while they pursued an idea that might be truly elegant, whether there was a use for it or not.

The other was the need to find a way for Taiwan to reunite with Mainland China without falling from the great wealth of the Island Economic Miracle to a bucolic nightmare in one generation. She tried to explain both these reasons to Larry Black:

"Well, Mr. Black, there are two reasons we care about the Galileo Model. The first reason is just because it is the simplest, most beautiful and sensitive way we know to represent the way people think in a precise way. And that's important, even if you can't find out any way to make use of it in your everyday life.

"But there's a second reason. The Galileo Space is the most useful way we've every discovered to help us understand how and why people do what they do, and to help change what they think and do."

And Lu Wi touched the computer keyboard again. This time, data less than a week old flashed onto the screen. On the right of the screen, they showed circles with the words "Bush," "Conservative," "Pro Life", "Foreign Affairs," and "Republican" on the right side of the screen. On the left side were circles labelled "Liberal," "Democrat," and closer to the middle, "Economic Recovery" and "Clinton." At the middle, slightly closer to Clinton than Bush, was the word "Honest." Toward the top left, almost at the margin of the picture, were circles labelled "Change," and "Perot."

Now Lu Wi pressed another key, and the map was filled with blue and red dots, each so small you could hardly see it, but they looked like clouds surrounding the first circles on the screen.

"Take a look at this space," Lu Wi said. "This space represents measurements made for the four days just before the presidential election," she said. "The blue dots represent the position men take relative to these candidates and issues. The red dots represent women's positions."

She paused to give everyone a chance to examine the pictures on the screen.

"Now, if you have the time to count up all these dots," she said... (the class laughed at the obvious impossibility) "you'll find that about 43% of them are closest to Clinton, 18% of them are closest to Perot, and about 39% are closest to George Bush."

"And," she continued, "if you don't have that much time or patience, you can run this little program called "count votes," -- which she then ran -- "and it would tell you this."

She pressed the return key, and, sure as Death and Taxes, the program wrote on the screen,

Clinton = 43%

Bush   = 39%

Perot = 18%

And it was pretty obvious why you would want to make a space like the Galileo. The Galileo space not only described how people thought and felt, *it described what they were going to do.*

Now how much would you pay? But wait, before you answer, in addition to these great knives, you also get...

Seriously, though, there was another trick you could do with a Galileo. Lu Wi pulled the map of the election space back onto the computer screen.

"Let's test out some of the strategies the candidates used."

She pressed the "F2" function key on her computer, and a window opened up. It asked her to list the concept she wanted to move, and she typed "Clinton." Then it asked her to lists a "target." Lu Wi explained that this was the place toward which you wanted to move the first concept (or Clinton, in this case). Lu Wi typed "Yourself."

"Candidates that are closest to the people's own position win the election," she said "So that's where we want to go."

The the computer asked her to list the message concepts. These were the issues that candidate was using to try to get elected. She typed

"Change", then "moderate," and "democrat." She pressed the "F5" key, and Galileo wrote some numbers on the screen. It said something like

"The distance between Clinton and Yourself is 62.4 units. Positioning near "Change,

Moderate and Democrat" will leave you 37.3 units from Yourself. This is 59.78% of the present distance."

"Holy expletive deleted!" Dewey said. "You can calculate the effect of a strategy *in advance*?" Dewey could see that, if that were true, the program could easily calculated the potential effects of *every possible strategy* faster than a speeding bullet, then report back the top ten or so most effective possible strategies. (Galileo already could do this, of course, as Dewey would have known if only he would have tried the option "Message Strategies" back at Hughes Aircraft.)

"Other factors equal," Lu Wi said.

"Professor Lu," Larry asked, "Could you use the Galileo to sell bicycles?"

"That's what it's mainly used for outside the universities," Lu Wi answered. "I mean, not for bicycles specifically, but to sell products."

Now, if this escapes you, please don't panic. I must say I'm from a civilization near the Galactic Core about a billion years more advanced than yours, but math was never my strong suit and I can't say I'm too clear on what Lu Wi was saying, even today. But it's enough for me to know you can actually do what she says. I've seen it done. Huey does it all the time. So, if your eyes glaze over trying to read stuff like the last few paragraphs, just skip them, close your eyes for a minute, and repeat as necessary, "Technobabble, technobabble, technobabble" until you feel better.

But you don't have to be a rocket scientist to know that those super-duper mathematical equations, and the hint of a computer program that solved them, pushed the already wavering Dewey right over the edge. He was hooked on Lu Wi big time. He asked her one more question:

"Professor, just where is this space? I mean, does it actually exist, or is it just a mathematical model?"

"Oh, it exists," Lu Wi said, "But it's not in any one particular place. The information that defines it is stored in people's brains."

"Like a computer memory?" Dewey asked.

"No, not like that at all," Lu Wi said. "Each of the objects represents a bunch of neurons in the brain that are active whenever a person is thinking of that object. And the 'distances' between any pair of objects is stored as the connection patterns in the brain's neural network. If two objects are seen to be very similar, then the neurons that represent them are very tightly connected in the brain. If they're very different, the connections are either weak or negative." (Technobable, Technobable, Technobable!)

Technobable to you, maybe, and certainly to me. But to Dewey, the word's "Neural network" rang like a loud bell.

Dewey's glands were in turbo overdrive, and his ability to hear, much less evaluate, what Lu Wi was saying was deeply impaired. By the end of the first evening (the class met once a week Wednesday night for three hours) Dewey had a dim idea what Lu Wi was going to cover in the class, and he was very excited. He was deeply impressed with Lu Wi's intelligence and command of her subject matter, and he found the topic to be fascinating. He couldn't wait to learn more, and the week until the next class seemed unwaitable. So he didn't wait. Next morning, Thursday, Dewey was in Lu Wi's office with a present.

Chapter 12: Notes on the First Class

Dewey's Notes:

> Lu Wi 267 MFAC-Fillmore
> (716) 555 2141
> Office Hours tt 1:30-2:30, w 6:00-7:00

Richard's notes:

> DuMond (keyboards)

Auto Mechanics notes:

> Check n-dimensional space, Riemann surfaces. Review tensors.

Larry's notes:

> Get W&F The Measurement of Communication Processes: Galileo Theory and Method, Academic Press, NY, 1980.

> Check prices on Galileo, Terra Research and Computing Co., Troy, NY? Detroit, MI? Get phone numbers.

Chapter 13: UB

Lu Wi looked up from her desk in MFAC-Fillmore, Millard Fillmore Academic Center, namesake of one of two US Presidents to die in Buffalo, New York, and home of the University at Buffalo Department of Communication. (One other president, William McKinley -- died in Buffalo, much more spectacularly, after having been shot by the anarchist Leon Colgosz. He died in a house which would later become a residence, then, still, later, a parking lot, at

Canisius High School, the only Jesuit high school in Buffalo.)

Located on the Joseph P. Ellicott Campus, the only campus at the University of Buffalo that looked remotely like a university campus, Lu Wi's office looked out across Marshall Court onto the Northwest shore of Lake LaSalle. At one end of the lake, connected to the shore by a picturesque arched bridge, lay Kanazawa Island. Slightly larger than a tennis court, Kanazawa Island was perhaps the smallest Island on the Green Hills of Earth to have a name.

The University of Buffalo had two campuses when Lu Wi, Dewey, Curly, The Chair, Larry and Richard, and, of course Huey, first met. At the corner of Main Street and Bailey Avenue in Buffalo, the traditional and quite beautiful South Campus was the original site of the old, private, University of Buffalo when Governor Nelson Rockefeller bought it for a dollar, placed it in the State University of New York (A.K.A. SUNY) and renamed it the *State University of New York at*

Buffalo, a name which never really caught on with anyone.

The State University of New York at that time consisted of 64 campuses around the State, and 350,000 students, making it the largest centrally administered university in the United States, and, since the demise of the Soviet Union, one of the largest remaining Planned Economies on the Green Hills of Earth. Four of these campuses were University Centers, which were designated as the centers for research and doctoral education in the system. Of these, The University *at* Buffalo (formerly called the University *of* Buffalo) was the largest and most complete. Alas, although each of these campuses was called *The State University of New York at ----*, each also preferred some other name, and it was a sure sign of an outsider to hear any of them called *The State University of New York At*.

In his zeal to make Buffalo the site of a new Berkeley, Rockefeller had built an entirely new campus two miles north of the original site, on a huge swamp in Amherst, NY. (Those present say that the Groundbreaking Ceremony was actually more like a Waterbreaking Ceremony.)

No one has ever been accused of actually *liking* the Amherst or North Campus, which consisted of a mile-long spine of connected brick buildings easily defended in case of student uprisings, none of which have ever occurred.

Just a mile north of the spine, actually a part of the Amherst Campus, lay a cluster of pueblo-like structures encircled and isolated from the rest of the world by Frontier Road on the East, North and West, and by the John James Audubon Parkway on the South. This cluster consisted of a combination of dormitory space, cafeterias, the Katherine Cornell Theatre, convenience stores, laundries, Ping-Pong tables, the Edward H. Letchworth Woods, canoes, reading rooms, a satellite library, a satellite computer center, classrooms, laboratories and faculty offices. It was meant as a complete habitat from which the student would seldom, if ever, have to emerge.

And a good thing, too, since, without a car, travelling to Anywhere from the isolated Amherst campus would be a truly daunting experience even for the hardiest hoofer. In the Cold Winds of Amherst in Winter, travel on foot could be life-threatening. Isolated though it may be, however, and unlike the rest of the Amherst Campus, the Ellicott Campus was quite beautiful.

The Department of Communication occupied the entire top floor of the Millard Fillmore Academic Center, and part of the second floor of Porter Hall. Bounded at the one end by the Chair's office and at the other by The Richard A. Holmes Jr. Memorial Computing Laboratory, the Department consisted of a long, wide central corridor running South (Holmes) to North (Chair). The East side of the corridor was made up of faculty and staff offices, all overlooking Marshall Court and Lake LaSalle. Along the West side were glass walls through which one could look down into the Satellite Computing Center (Chair side) and the Satellite Library (Holmes Side). At the Center of the West side was the main entrance, and about 50 feet South of the entrance, was the Seminar Room in which Lu Wi's class met. The Seminar Room had a white board along the North wall, a blackboard along the East wall, and nothing along the West wall. The South wall was actually a glass wall looking down onto the Satellite Library.

(Neither the Satellite Library nor the Satellite Computing Center had anything to do with satellites, but were so named to indicate that they were subsidiary to the Main Library at Lockwood Hall and the Main Computing Center at Fronczak Hall, both a mile away at the Spine.)

Specifically remodeled to the Communication Department's specifications, the top floor of MFAC was Good Space. Due to the failure of trickle down economics, the savings and loan scandal, poor fiscal policies and a generally bad worldwide economic climate, however, the Department suffered an abrupt and unexpected 100% Downward Adjustment in its furnishing budget just as the remodeling was completed, and had had to furnish the entire space with stuff from University Surplus.

As a result that Good Space looked a lot like low income housing in Eastern Europe. There were no carpets, no art, no decoration of any kind save for a few plants the Chair's Secretary had kindly provided. Like the rest of the University at Buffalo, and like the Mighty Buffalo Bills, who had made it to the Super Bowl the last two years only to fall before first the New York (Jersey?) Giants then the Washington Redskins, that Good Space just couldn't seem to make it over the final hurdle to becoming Great Space.

Such was the setting for Lu Wi and Dewey's first private meeting.

Chapter 14:

Lu Wi, Dewey and SPOT

"Mr. DuMond?" she asked. "What can I do for you?"

"I, uh, I ... was very interested in some of the things you said last night, Professor Wi," Dewey said.

"Lu,", Lu Wi said. "Professor Lu. In China, the first name comes last and the last name comes first," she said.

"Oh!, uh, Oh, I'm sorry, I..."

"That's all right, Mr. DuMond. Don't worry about it."

"Dewey,", Dewey said. "Please, call me Dewey. Everyone does. I mean, I'm sorry, I..."

"Then call me Lu Wi," Lu Wi said. "Everyone does."

They both laughed, and Lu Wi gestured at a seat next to her desk.

Lu Wi felt a spreading warmth when Dewey entered her office. He was a tall, well-muscled man, perhaps her age or maybe a few years younger (terribly difficult to guess the age of Europeans, Lu Wi thought!), and Lu Wi had gone a long time longer than she cared to recall without ... .

"Please sit down, Dewey, and tell me what's on your mind."

Dewey began to blurt out the Story of His Life. He explained that he was a Computer Science major at UB, had graduated and worked as a computer programmer at Hughes Aircraft, ran a small business in computer games, which he mainly wrote, and had come back to UB because life as a corporate engineer wasn't as fulfilling as he planned, and he had taken her course because it was going to deal with Neural Networks, which he had found fascinating, even though it wasn't in the Computer Science Department, and that it also dealt with Galileos, and he was supposed to install a Galileo System at Hughes Aircraft before he left, and didn't believe much in social science, but what she had said last night seemed to be, like, uh, Really Scientific, and he had, uh, brought her sort of a present...(but he didn't mention that his fiancée had croaked abruptly on impact with a bridge in Washington, that he was rejected by the Piano

Performance Program at the Department of Music, or that he was biting the heel of his hand on the way to her office.)

Lu Wi, who was a human being like the rest of you (but not me), heard mainly a blur of words, but a few of them stood out. The words "computer programmer" and "Hughes Aircraft" and "Computer Science" and "I mainly wrote" socked her right in a place Dewey had scrutinized earlier.

Truth be told (and I'll tell it here, I promise you, Huey) Lu Wi had been extremely disappointed in Buffalo. First of all, John Hopkins bought computers like everyone else bought notepads. Money was abundant, since Hopkins was at the Core of the Establishment Medical Community, and federal money flowed through it like water through the Mighty Niagara River. She'd worked on a $35 million renewable grant in the Communication Program there, and when she found out the level of Peanuts that came out of Nelson Rockefeller's Berkeley of the East, (as people were wont to call the University at

Buffalo) it brought real tears to her eyes. Great Gosh Almighty, the Richard A. Holmes, Jr. Memorial Computing Center had half a dozen Apple II's still in service!

There was not one single Computer Programmer on the staff of the Communication Department, and, to add insult to injury, the two foremost Galileo theorists on the Green Hills of Earth had become Honorable Ancestors only weeks ago. "Shit", she said to herself, (but delicately, and gently.)

Truth be told, the University at Buffalo was only one of the world's great institutions that were struggling with the deep and fundamental changes not just the US but the world was experiencing at the end of the Second Millenium (Western Calendar).

Most dramatic of these changes was the precipitous collapse of Planned Economies everywhere. And most spectacular of these was the demise of what had been called "The Soviet Union." (General Motors could lay claim to a fairly spectacular Adjustment as well, and was losing about $1,000,000 an hour on this very day.) The collapse of the Red Menace was not only spectacular, but it was a positive proof that the kinds of concepts Humanity had developed to understand itself were clearly inadequate to deal with the complexities of a Totally Post Modern Worldwide Communication System, in which money and information flowed at light speed across national borders with the unstoppable ebullience of a fart in church.

Consider this: In the crude pre-Galileo spatial analogy humanity had devised to understand politics, the Soviet Union stood foursquare on the Far Left. To the Right were the Capitalists, led by the Running Dog Imperialist United States (a term beloved by the Chinese Communists, particularly Mau Zedong). But -- think of this! -- when the Soviets began to totter, liberals and radicals in the Soviet Union, who wanted to move toward a Capitalist model on the right, where considered the Soviet Union's political left, while conservatives, who wanted to stay on the left, were called "rightists." The leftists prevailed, at least at first, and so the Soviet Union plunged to the Left, into the waiting arms of the Rightist Capitalists.

Those who wanted to think clearly about what was happening had only one choice: they had to abandon the old concepts and develop a more powerful way of thinking.

Lu Wi was one of these, and her model was the Galileo model. Galileo Space didn't allow journalists and politicians to assign places at their whim in the Space, but relied entirely on carefully made measurements. (Those of you who don't think it's possible to measure these kinds of things probably don't have your own computer yet. Better hurry -- the world is passing you by!)

And the Galileo Space didn't only have a Left and a Right. It had an Up and a Down and a Front and a Back and a Hither, Thither and Yon as well. And as many dimensions as the measurements called for. True, no one. could picture this complicated space in their mind, but the realities of Third Millenium Humanity just refused to be crammed into a mental model small enough to fit inside one person's mind.

But it fit nicely into a computer's, thank you, and Huey, as it turned out, had pretty much the world's total computer network to draw on. Huey didn't quite exist yet, but Lu Wi and Dewey were very close to giving him birth.

"So you're a computer programmer, Mr. DuMond?" she asked.

"Dewey,", Dewey said. He explained that he did indeed program computers, and that he was Extremely Good At It, but that he was actually a Computer Scientist, not a simple programmer, and he was Deeply Interested in the Very Scientific Stuff Lu Wi was teaching in her seminar. And he told her that he would program anything she wanted, first rate, world class, all she had to do was ask. And he had brought her a small gift.

When you visit someone in Asia, you bring your host a gift. In Korea or Japan (which has the largest per capita consumption of alcohol of any nation on earth,) you bring a quart of Johnny Walker Red Label to a High Status Person, or maybe a carton of Marlboros. You wouldn't ordinarily bring a present to a Woman, but Lu Wi was not an ordinary Asian Woman.

In China, you would bring a gift, along with a carefully prepared booklet that accompanied the gift. This booklet usually consisted of about a dozen pages of white paper, about the size of your hand, with a two inch strip of red paper attached from top to bottom of the middle of the cover. The booklet itself would be contained in a cardboard case with the same kind of decoration. Inside the booklet would be the highest name of the giver, along with an elegant description of the gift. Your host (a man, of course) could accept the gift, or return it with no offense to the giver, if he didn't need or want it.

Dewey didn't know any of this, but the bringing of a gift, as luck would have it, was exactly The Right Thing To Do, and Lu Wi was very pleased.

I said earlier that Lu Wi could, in an earlier era, have been Queen of China but I didn't tell you she would have rejected that honor if she could. Any noble woman would. You see, women never meant beans in Asia, and the Queen would have been nothing to look up to. (Confucius, like Socrates, Plato and Aristotle, believed women somewhat less than humans, and thought of them as domestic animals, like dogs and cats.) She would have been locked in the Palace, forbidden to go out and even to see her own relatives, and the King would have had as many as nine other wives, thirty six others that were called wives, and a great number of concubines that would be called neither queen nor wife.

The children of all these women would be raised as children of the Queen, and would have called the Queen their mother. The King's first born male would be successor to the throne, regardless of which of these women bore him,

Queen or no Queen. The ranking consort would have sat at table with the King. Lu Wi would have barfed in her ricebowl.

Now, Lu Wi was a Chinese woman, with a Ph.D., in Buffalo, New York, and it may be a little hard for Westerners to realize how exceptional that would have been only a few years ago. Not long ago, a Chinese official would have refused posting to a foreign country if he could possibly get out of it, just as China would have rejected visits from any foreigners.

In 1557, in return for military assistance against pirates, the Viceroy of the Province of Koangtong (as it was then called) allowed the Portuguese to establish a permanent colony on the peninsula of Macao. If Dewey had been born in that year, he would have lived almost his entire life before any Portuguese entered China, which he could have seen from his window on Macao. In 1578, the Chinese allowed the Portuguese to visit Canton, China, twice a year. On those trips, they could go ashore, set up marts and emporiums to trade merchandise from India and Japan, but they had to go back to their ships each night. The Chinese didn't cotton to strangers, Pardner, No Siree.

Lu Wi was a New Woman, the harbinger of a New China, a woman who had traveled ten thousand miles to a new country, a woman with a Doctorate, the highest degree a Chinese Man could aspire to, a woman in a foreign land, and when Dewey brought her a gift, no matter what her mind told her, her emotions tingled like Dewey's sex glands.

"You brought me a gift?" she asked.

"It's nothing, really," he said, which was about as nearly correct and polite as he could have been even if he knew what he was doing.

"It's just something I came across at Hughes," he said. "It's an artificial neural network program called SPOT," he said.

The name "SPOT" struck a responsive chord with Lu Wi, but, not sure, she said,

"SPOT? What's SPOT?"

Dewey tried his best to explain SPOT to Lu Wi. He understood SPOT very well, to be sure, but he wasn't completely himself as he tried to explain. He stumbled through the concept of a supervised network, with a "teacher" that knew the right answer and "corrected" the network every time it tried an answer that wasn't completely right. He explained how the network rewired itself to get closer to the right answer each time it dropped the ball. He didn't do his best, because his mouth was too dry and Lu Wi was just too damned attractive.

But Lu Wi understood in spite of his clumsiness. And she knew a lot more than Dewey did about how minds worked. A lot more.

Chapter 15: Second Class

Lu Wi's second class was better than the first. The students were more comfortable, and, after a week to consider what they had to learn here, came back with a real interest. Lu Wi reviewed what she presented the last week. She reminded them again about "objects," and drew from them their own recollections of what objects were.

"How about a tappet?" she asked. "Is a tappet an object?"

"You bet!" said one of the mechanics.

"And a very important object at that!" said the other brother.

(Lu Wi had done her homework. How many Ph.D.s have the slightest idea what a tappet is, or that an auto mechanic would know and care about it?)

"And how about a Griffin?"

"A Griffin is a mystical beast with the head of a lion and the body of an Eagle," Richard said. Richard had done his undergraduate work at Canisius College, the home of the Golden Griffins. Lu Wi had done more homework than the students!

"But is it an object?" Lu Wi asked.

"Sure it is," Richard said. "If you can think of it, it's an object."

"Does an object have to be a real, material thing?" she asked.

"An object can be anything you can think about," Larry, the bicycle maker, Richard's father, said. "It doesn't have to be a material thing."

"Can a person be an object?" Lu Wi asked.

"Why not?" one of the mechanics said.

"My Brother is an object," the other mechanic said, "An object of ridicule."

Everybody laughed. (The class soon learned that the mechanic brothers could break out into five or ten minutes of pretty funny material if Lu Wi didn't stop them, and lots of times she didn't.)

"And what is an object?" she asked again.

"That depends," said Richard.

"What does it depend on?" Lu Wi asked.

"It depends on who's looking at it, and when and where they're looking at it." he answered.

"My God, you people are good!" Lu Wi said.

She was elated. When she had first found there were only four people registered in her class, she was disappointed. She would have had to get special permission from the Chair to continue the class with fewer than five students. (He would have given her the Moon if she wanted it, but she didn't know that yet, and probably never would.) When Dewey registered late and made five, she was relieved. But the responsiveness and intelligence of this class was bouying her spirits. Not many classes, anywhere, have five first class students in them. At this level, students come in Ones.

"And how's your wife?" Lu Wi asked.

This time they were stumped, and no one answered. They all immediately presented the "I'm thinking about this real hard and I hope someone else will answer soon but *please* don't call on me because I don't have a clue" look on their faces. Every good student masters this look early in their scholastic career.

"I can see you're not familiar with the eminent American Philosopher H. Youngman," Lu Wi said.

But the mechanics were.

"Compared to what?" one brother said.

"Take my wife, *Please*!" the other called out.

"Aha! You know who he is!" Lu Wi said.

"Doctor, it hurts when I do this," one brother said, raising his hand in a distorted way.

"Then don't do that!" said the other mechanic.

"I'm afraid you'll need an operation."

"I'd like a second opinion."

"You're ugly, too!"

"Doctor, will I be able to play the Violin after this operation?"

"Of course you will!"

"Wonderful! I always wanted to play the violin!"

"Ok! Ok!" said Lu Wi. "You Know who he is! But do you know what he means?"

There was a long silence, and the Old Man spoke.

"He means that a Jew in a concentration camp is different from a Jew on TV," Larry said.

He surprised himself when he said it, and he brought the class to a sudden stop. In nearly forty years, he had never, ever, mentioned anything about what he had seen at Buchenwald, and he hadn't a clue as to why it popped out of his mouth now. The mechanic brothers didn't say anything else funny for a long time, but Lu Wi's point was made.

Finally Richard moved the class along.

"It means that nothing has a meaning all by itself. Everything has a meaning in the situation you find it in. I've seen tigers in zoos more than once, but one time I saw a tiger on a leash comin' out of an elevator I was waitin' for in the lobby of a hotel I was playin' in Mexico City and, Great Gosh Almighty, it was something different from any tiger I ever saw before. I mean, like, Man, I was, like *two feet away* from it, and it was Awesome!" (Dewey found out as he got to be his friend that Richard was a deeply religious man, and would never, never, say "God" in a trivial way.)

Lu Wi would have preferred that the conversation go on, but the remark about the concentration camp had a chilling effect on the dialogue. Lu Wi filled the silence with a short lecture on how every object had a meaning relative to every other object, and how you could measure the meaning of objects by telling how different each object was from other relevant objects on some sort of numerical scale, but Dewey couldn't completely pay attention. He'd ask her later what she said. What he heard (Wonder of Wonders for a flash Computer Scientist and Engineer, magna cum laude graduate of the UB Computer Science

Department and Hughes Aircraft alumnus) was "Technobabble, technobabble, technobabble!"

But things improved rapidly. Lu Wi introduced SPOT to the class, and they loved it. The auto mechanics were very bright and very quick. They understood in seconds that SPOT could learn more than conversations, and soon were discussing how they could teach SPOT to diagnose problems in Auto Mechanics, just as Dewey had taught SPOT to call offensive plays in football.

"You could feed it symptoms, then tell it what the problem was!" the first mechanic said.

"And you could test it on a different set of problems and see if it knew what it was talking about!" said the second.

"We could fire our Service Manager back at the Garage!"

"No, we can't do that, he's the one who knows how to read!"

(Over the next two weeks, they trained SPOT to be a Damned Fine Service Manager.)

"Could you teach it to design Bicycles and Roller Skates?" Larry asked.

"I don't see why not," Dewey answered. "But I don't know enough about Bicycles to know how to do it. Or Roller Skates."

"My Daddy does," Richard said. "My Daddy knows more about Bicycles and Roller Skates than any man alive," he said.

Now, designing bicycles and roller skates turned out to be a mite harder than diagnosing car problems. The two mechanics from Boston had SPOT trained better than a Chilton's manual in a week and a half, but it took Larry and Richard nearly all semester to get SPOT to be halfway useful as a bicycle and roller skate designer. They fed in information about tensile strengths and weights and costs of materials, coefficients of friction of chains and gears, gear ratios, angles of forks and seat suspensions, tubing diameters and composition strengths and, technobabble, technobabble, technobabble, by Christmas break, SPOT was pretty good at least at answering questions that helped Larry and Richard design bicycles and roller skates.

But then, Lu Wi introduced a new technology to the class that put Dewey into The Zone. Computer programmers know what The Zone is, although they may call it by different names. (Richard A. Holmes, Jr., the namesake of the Richard A Holmes, Jr. Memorial Computing Center at the Department of Communication at the University at Buffalo, called it the "Programmer's Trance," but it meant the same as "The Zone.")

She taught them about CATPAC.

(This is Roscoe interrupting the flow of this story. I mean, like, I'm no rocket scientist, and I can't understand half the stuff I'm telling you, readers -- hell, half is pretty generous, I don't understand *any* of it. But I promised Huey I'd tell it all to you, and I'm just reciting words I memorized, and I don't know what the **** I'm talking about. I hope you do. Just keep repeating, over and over, "Technobabble, technobabble, technobabble...")

Let me try to explain Catpac. CATPAC is another kind of artificial neural network. Just like SPOT and ROVER, it can read words. But, for SPOT and ROVER, you give them a word or phrase, then give them another one which is what you want them to say whenever they see the first phrase, or something like the first phrase. So you say "Good Morning, SPOT," and you tell SPOT to tell you "Buenas Dias, Senor!" and it learns to do this.

But with CATPAC, you just give it something to read and it reads it. Anything. The phone book. The Bible. The Loves of Casanova. And, while it reads it, it figures out how to put those words, or at least the most important words, into a Galileo Space.

Dewey says the way it works is super easy, but I'm not sure I understand it. I promised to tell all, so I'll repeat the explanation here, but, to tell the truth, I can't see why you need to know any of this technical stuff. If you don't care how it works, just skip the next two paragraphs, recite "Technobabble" a few more times, and go on to the paragraph that starts with a "*."

Everytime CATPAC reads an important word (CATPAC dumps words like "a", "the", "for", and that before it starts, and then keeps track only of the words that occur most often) it turns on a neuron that corresponds to that word. It reads words five or seven or whatever at a time, so there will always be five or seven or whatever neurons turned on at any given time.

Now, when these five or seven neurons are all turned on at the same time, CATPAC tightens up the connection among them, just like Pavlov's dogs developed a connection between the sound of a bell ringing and food, so that they'd drool whenever they heard the bell. By the time CATPAC is done reading whatever it read, it makes a Galileo Space where words that usually came close to each other in the text were close to each other in the Galileo Space. (Well, I guess it wasn't so bad, after all!)

   * (Start here if you didn't read the last two paragraphs!) This kind of neural network, Dewey says, is called a "self-organizing" or "unsupervised" neural network, because, unlike SPOT and ROVER, nobody tells it what to think or what to say. It makes up its own "mind" just by reading. The more it reads, the more it knows.

   Now CATPAC isn't as smart as you or me, and maybe not even as smart as ROVER, who you'll meet in a few minutes. But I'll tell you one thing about CATPAC, I mean that good old boy can read like a demon, and he/she/it never, and I mean *never* gets eyestrain.

   Dewey's mind was deep in the possibilities of a computer program that could learn by itself and had to shake himself to listen to Lu Wi when she said

"Can you come to my office after class, Mr. DuMond? I have a present for you!"

Chapter 16: Notes on the Second Class

Dewey's notes:

CATPAC makes Galileo a new ball game. CATPAC on the Internet...check with Computing Center...

The Mechanics' notes:

How's your wife?
Compared to what?

Sound's like backpropagation to me.

There must be a better supervised network than SPOT. Let's find out.

Richard's notes:

Larry's Notes:

Can CATPAC work with a scanner? Does everything have to be typed in?

Chapter 17: ROVER

It was late -- about 10:15 P.M. -- and dark when Dewey walked into Lu Wi's office. Lu Wi's room was only dimly lit by a small lamp on her desk. In the warm glow of the lamp, Lu Wi was even more beautiful than she was in the harsh overhead fluorescent lights of the Seminar Room. Had he been thinking about Deep Philosophical Issues, the flush of tingling sensations that swept over him would have reminded him again that his own personal consciousness was not running his whole show. As it was, those sensations just made him, temporarily, a little stupid.

"I, uh, ... what can I do for you, Professor Lu?" he asked.

"I had a great time playing with SPOT," Lu Wi said, "but I thought it sounded familiar when you gave it to me. So I looked around a bit, and, do you know, Dewey, SPOT was written here in this Department!"

"Really? I thought it came from someplace in Eastern New York."

"Maybe the commercial version. But the first scientific versions were written here. Take a look."

Lu Wi handed Dewey a disk. On it was written in longhand, with a ball point pen,

SPOT and ROVER: source code
8/27/92.

What caught Dewey's eye first and hard was the phrase "source code." Dewey had a commercial version of SPOT, which is what the thin wristed, pale complexion community (computer programmers don't get out in the sunshine much) calls "executable" code. You can use it, but you can't actually read the program, or see how it's written. Programs are written first in a source code, which has to be compiled and linked into a code which computers can understand (but people can't). With the source code (SPOT was written in FORTRAN), Dewey could find out exactly how SPOT worked. He could even revise it.

He was so taken by this gift of SPOT source code that it took him a moment to notice the word "ROVER."

"What's a ROVER?" he asked.

"ROVER is SPOT's smarter brother," Lu Wi said.

"Smarter?"

"Here, take a look." She gestured for Dewey to sit beside her at her computer. Dewey felt her arm brush his, then her leg against his leg. Trouble, trouble, trouble, right here in River City, his semi-conscious consciousness mumbled. He looked across at her, only inches from him, and, with a mighty effort, did not stare at her tiny but exquisite breasts.

"This is SPOT," she said, and pulled a diagram onto the screen. It showed a layer of input neurons connected to a layer of hidden neurons, which, in turn, was connected to a layer of output neurons.

"Letters and words go in the input layer, jiggle around in the hidden layer, then come out different letters and words in the output layer."

"Gotcha," Dewey said. He knew this, of course, since he had explained SPOT to LU Wi only a week ago.

"Now watch," she said. She called up SPOT, and typed to it:

"Sit down, SPOT."

SPOT said "Yes, Boss."

She typed again

"Sit down, SPOT."

And SPOT said "Yes, Boss."

Again and again, she typed

"Sit down, SPOT," and, again and again, SPOT said

"Yes, Boss."

Dewey got the point. In a lot of ways, SPOT seemed very human. But no human being would respond in the same way to the same input over and over, without change, forever. But SPOT would.

Next, Lu Wi called up Rover. She typed

"Sit down, Rover."

ROVER said "Yes, Boss."

Lu Wi typed "Sit down, ROVER."

And ROVER said "I am sitting, Boss."

Lu Wi typed "Roll over, ROVER."

And ROVER said

"You got it, Babe."

She typed again "Roll over, ROVER."

And ROVER said "Again, redundant one?"

"Great Gosh Almighty!" Dewey said.

Even if Dewey's mind hadn't been impaired by sex hormones, he would still have been stunned. Rover could understand *exactly the same words* in different ways depending on the context in which it heard them.

"ROVER's context sensitive?" he asked?

"And more than that," Lu Wi said. "Watch."

She pulled up another diagram onto the screen, which looked exactly like SPOT. Dewey noticed only one difference. From the output neurons were drawn a set of connections back to some of the input neurons.

"Of course!" he said. "Of course!" SPOT can only read what you say. It hasn't a clue about what it says itself. But ROVER *knows what it says!*"

Lu Wi and Dewey exchanged a lot of technobabble for a few minutes, about objective self awareness and seeing oneself as an object and definition of self and George Herbert Mead and a lot of other stuff I can't recall, but it all meant one thing that was, truth be told, Pretty Special:

In a very, very, *very* crude and limited way, ROVER was self-conscious.

Chapter 18: The Third Class

If you thought the second class was exciting, Lu Wi's third session just about nailed everybody to the wall. The mechanics played the Devil's advocate and argued brilliantly that ROVER wasn't self aware in the way a human being was. They pointed out that it was completely predictable if you knew how it had been trained, had no humor, didn't laugh or cry, had no goals or dreams, was never happy or disappointed, and didn't even care if it lived or died.

Dewey held his ground. He said that ROVER had a very limited brain indeed, with only a few hundred neurons and only a few thousand connections, while a human being had somewhere near a hundred billion neurons, with each one connected to about a thousand other ones. He pointed out that ROVER had no eyes, no ears, no hands or feet, no skin, no taste buds, no nose, and so its inputs were totally predictable and shallow. What if it had all these inputs, wouldn't it's little mind be so complicated no programmer could ever know what it was going to say or think at any time?

And what if it had some circuits in it that connected its internal voltages and neural connections to it in a way that it suffered problems if things didn't go its way, but felt better when things worked out better. Wouldn't it have goals and feelings then?

He showed how the simple 486 chip in Lu Wi's computer had to do everything one thing at a time, or serially, but a chemical brain did everything at once, in parallel. Hell, even a bee had about a million neurons and could process at about 5 gigaflops (A technobabble term from computer science that meant a bee brain could perform about 5 billion operations a second) while ROVER only had a few hundred neurons and a top speed of about only 10 MIPS (another technical term that some computer scientists think means "million instructions per second" and which others claim means "meaningless indicator of processor speed.")

Of course, ROVER couldn't even begin to compete with a real human brain, and never would. But, in principle, it worked the same way. (To a scientist, principles are everything, and Dewey was, after all, at least a rookie scientist.) And, what's more, with the incredible growth in computer technology, ROVERS a thousand times as smart as their own ROVER were only a few years away, even if no new improvements in ROVER'S design were made. If you were to move to the newest VLSI (very large scale integration) analog chips that were as they spoke being designed and even built, you could make a ROVER that actually ran in parallel instead of one operation at a time like the 486 ROVER. And, Great Gosh Almighty, with new biotechnology on the drawing board, you could abandon silicon altogether and make an artificial neural network out of real biological neurons.

In the end the brothers admitted that, in principle, they agreed with him and were only arguing for the sake of hammering out the truth. They talked for a long time more about the meanings of this kind self-conscious machine. Just what was consciousness, anyway? Was there a place in your brain you could call your "mind", where "you" were?

How smart did a ROVER have to get before you had to treat it with respect? How smart did a ROVER have to get before it had legally protected civil rights? How smart did a ROVER have to get before it was murder to turn it off?

And what if you linked two ROVERS together. Would they be one big ROVER, or still two ROVERS? How tightly did you have to link them together until they blended into one ROVER? Or maybe two ROVERS linked together made *three* ROVERS -- the two original ROVERS plus a third, new SUPER ROVER? What about two people linked together -- or 1 billion or five billion people linked together? What about the growing satellite communication system, fibre optic cables, the worldwide computer network that was growing faster than the national debt? Could the *whole world* become self conscious? What would happen to individual freedom if humanity as a whole became a self-conscious SUPER ROVER?

At the end of the three-hour class, everyone was pretty well burned out from the intensity, and the conversation wore down.

"So, do we think ROVER is a person?" Lu Wi asked.

And Larry, the bicycle and roller skate maker and the only one among them who had ever seen the inside of a concentration camp, said:

"White, black, yellow, Jew, Arab, you know, all these people turn out in the end to be the same. It doesn't really matter if he's made out of meat or he's made out of silicon, Professor Lu. If he's a person, then God loves him."

Chapter 19: Notes

Dewey's Notes:

Check VLSI analog chips; check biochips -- any hope soon?
Call Hughes.

Richard's notes:

Feedback circuit makes real music possible. SPOT is useless, because it can't hear itself sing. Music is played with the ear. Rover can hear itself. Check with Dewey.

The mechanics' notes:

Larry's notes:

Can a bicycle learn to ride itself? Can roller skates learn to keep you from falling?

Lu Wi's notes:

VLSI analog chips; biotech chips, phone home.

Chapter 20: Richard

  After class Larry's son Richard stopped Dewey on the way out.

  "Hey Dewey, I understand you're a fair keyboard player," he said.

  "I used to play around town," Dewey said, "But I'm afraid my chops are a bit rusty now."

"You want to go out and play some music, Man?"

It was 10:00 P.M. on a Wednesday night, and Dewey had been Out of Town for years. While work at 8:00 A.M. every day at Hughes had made him into a day person, he was quickly slipping back into Musicians' Hours here in the Queen City, and he really didn't feel much like going back to his apartment in Getzville to catch Whoopi's show yet another night.

"You may be disappointed, Richard, but, hell, I'll sit and watch, anyway."

Dewey followed Richard's car along the 190 Expressway into Downtown Buffalo. Dewey hadn't actually been in Buffalo since he'd come back from the City of the Angels; his whole life on the Niagara Frontier revolved around Amherst, where UB was, and Getzville, where he lived. When he went out, he usually went for some quiet drinks and Beef on Weck (a sandwich made out of steamed or roast beef, rich juice, and a Kümmelweck bun, which Dewey had never seen outside the Queen City area) at the Crows Nest, or to Elmo's for Wings and Genny Cream Ale, or to the Sweet Home Cafe for Heavy Metal and Tanqueray and Schweppes. (The Sweet Home Cafe was close enough to make it home if he had a tad too much Tanqueray.)

They parked and walked into the Lafayette Tap Room, where a small bandstand was set up just next to the entrance at the front of a long barroom/lounge. A quartet was playing straight-ahead jazz, and Dewey recognized the keyboard player from his own days on similar stands. He'd even played here a time or two himself. Dewey couldn't remember the player's name, since he really never got into the jazz scene, although he'd played some -- he was mainly a rock musician himself. But they both waved, and later he stopped by the bar for a drink with him and Richard.

"You want a drink, Man? I'm buying!" Richard said.

Dewey noticed that Richard picked up a new accent when he entered the Lafayette. At UB he spoke like an announcer on National Public Radio.

"Sure, I'll drink a beer. What about you?"

"Don't drink, man. No drugs, no smoke, no alcohol, this body's a temple!" Richard laughed. "I'll have some tonic water."

"Boy, this brings back some memories!" Dewey said.

"You been here?"

"I used to live in Buffalo. I played this room once or twice," Dewey answered.

"What you play, Man?"

"Rock and roll, Richard. Just Rock and Roll."

"You're singin' my song, Man," Richard said. "And call me 'Dick.' That's what my friends call me."

"You got it, Dick," Dewey said.

"Hey Dewey, what you think of that stuff we're doin' in Professor Lu's class. Is that a gas, or what?"

"Hey, I thought I'd just be passing the time till I could get in the Music Department, but

I'm freaking out, Man. That's some weird stuff! What do you think?

"ROVER blows me away, Man! I mean, last week, If you'd have asked me if there was a way to make anything like ROVER I'd have said it was impossible. Now, in one night I learned enough to know how to do it myself!"

"ROVER is a heavyweight, no doubt about it," Dewey said. He told Richard about how he had taught SPOT to call football plays, and how a simple change like the feedback loop could make such a tremendous difference. But the biggest thing Dewey had learned in the last week was CATPAC, and he told Richard so.

"The thing about CATPAC is it doesn't need to be trained," Dewey said. "I mean, it learns by itself. It's the way I learned my chops, Man. I mean, I never really had a teacher, but I picked up things from guys I played with, and copied what they did. Hell, all my best licks are stolen!"

"Yours and everybody else, my Man!" Richard said.

"Can you imagine CATPAC out on the Internet?" Dewey asked.

"What's the Internet?" Richard answered.

"The Internet, man. Its the network that ties all the university, military and corporate computers together. There's over 700,000 computers connected to it. UB is a main port. Can you imagine if CATPAC could wander around through those 700,000 computers and databases and what else and just read itself silly?"

"Yo, Baby! I know what that is. Jane works on that everyday. He's logged onto most of those computers himself, I bet." Richard said.

"Who's Jane?" Dewey asked.

"Jane's my Old Man," Richard said. "John Neumann, J.N., *Jane*. He works at the Computing Center at UB. And My Man Jane is the Network Man!"

"Holly Moley!" Dewey said. "Your Old Man is in charge of network services at UB?"

"You bet, Old Buddy. Jane is the Man Himself!"

"And he could get us out on the Network?"

"Hellfire, Man, you don't need Jane to go out on the Network. Anybody at UB can go out on Internet. Internet's *free*, Man!"

"Free?" (Nothing was ever free at Hughes Aircraft.)

"Yeah, Man. Free. Hey, Listen. What you care about that stuff for? You got the hots for that Chinese lady?"

The object of Dewey's affection turned his complexion from white to rosy red, instantly.

"I see, I see, you don't have to answer, My Man."

"I, uh, I..." Dewey stammered.

"Hey, don't sweat, My Friend. I don't want to poke my nose into your business. She' really a smart Lady, and y'all be a lucky man if you can get next to her, Yessiree!"

"Hell, Man. I mean, I got to say, like, I mean, I wouldn't kick her out of bed, you know. But I mean I didn't come to the class just to get laid, you know, I mean, I'm an engineer and I'm pretty much into this stuff." He was so unconvincing he wasn't even convincing himself. He tried to wriggle off the hook: " What brings you to the class, Dick? You not interested in that fine woman, are you?"

"Ha, Ha, Ha, DuMond, My Man, You real funny, yessiree, Real Funny! You know darn well that sweet lady is the wrong kind of person for me. She a little too ... *female*, you know? No Sir, I take one class every semester in whatever seems interesting. It's somethin' I picked up from my Daddy. He been takin' one class every semester since 1946!"

"1946!"

"That's right, Man. My Daddy is probably the best-educated man in the Queen City!"

"He must be!" (Richard never said so, but if his Daddy was the best-educated man in the Queen City, Richard himself was well on his way to being Number 2.)

"You work with him in the Bike Shop?"

"And roller skates, Man. We're partners -- Black and Son. I'm Son! But that's just my day job. At night, I'm a musician. Hell, man, I'm a Star!"

"A Star?"

"You'll see, you'll see. At midnight it's my turn. And in the Queen City, I am, I say, I am the Undiluted Queen of Rock and Roll!"

Dewey bought another round. He had to be quiet for a moment, because the conversation had covered a lot of emotional ground. He hadn't realized his feelings for Lu Wi were so obvious. Christ, they weren't even obvious to *him*.

Richard interrupted his reverie.

"You think you could teach ROVER to play music, Man?" Richard asked.

Dewey thought about that for about eight seconds, and his eyes lit up.

"Hell yes," he said. "Why not?"

Just then the quartet wound up its set, and Dewey's old acquaintance stopped by to get reacquainted. He already knew Richard. Meanwhile Richard moved to the bandstand to help set up. He disappeared for a while, then came back in costume. He laid a lace-cuffed hand on the keyboard player's shoulder.

"Hey man, can we hang onto your ax for a set or two? We got a slight problem here."

"Sure. I got to play here tomorrow anyway. I'll catch you then. Nice to see you again, Dewey!" He shook hands again with Dewey and went back to packing up.

"Hey Man," Richard said, "I got a slight problem here. My horn player ain't gonna show tonight. Seems he fought the Law and the Law won."

"I can't play horn, Dick."

"You can play keyboards, No?"

"Sure."

"Can you fake some horn chorus on Little Richard songs?"

"Can a stove cook?"

And so, after a magna cum laude degree in engineering and a tour in the City of Angels as a hot shot, fat salaried engineer at Hughes aircraft, Dewey found himself, less than a month after returning to the Queen City of the Great Lakes, back on the stage of the Lafayette Tap Room standing behind an ugly old Roland Synthesizer, inhaling blue smoke that hung everywhere around him, smelling like a bottle of used beer, and knocking out horn chorus rhythms behind the Undiluted Queen of Rock and Roll, Buffalo Edition. Richard might not have been The Man Himself, but he could fool you, yes he could, and Little Richard (the Original) was the very man whose music made Dewey want to quit his job at Topps Friendly Market and play some rock and roll in the first place. Does water seek its own level, or what? Even as he played, though, he made a mental note: *get Dick to introduce me to Jane!*

A womp bomp a lumop, a womp bam boom!

Chapter 21: Lu Wi and Dewey Sprint Toward Huey

Thursday Morning Dewey missed completely, and, when he woke up early Thursday afternoon, his ears still rang with the sound of Richard's vocals. Damn, he thought, that felt good. You can take the boy out of the band, but you can't take the band out of the boy, he thought. For the first time in half a year, he got out of bed with a sense of excitement.

Half of that was because of ROVER and CATPAC. Another half was because of Richard and good old rock and roll music, it's only rock and roll but I like it, give me that rock and roll music, any old time you use it, rock and roll never forgets! And the third half, larger than the other two halves (shut up, engineer brain, I can have three halves if I want) was the image of Lu Wi in his brain.

Now most of you have had a great sexual experience, your first, or your best, or your latest, or whatever, and it keeps on running through your mind and it never dims over years and decades. But the deepest, most intense sexual encounter Dewey could remember -- in fact the only one he found in his mind at all -- was the week before when Lu Wi had let her arm touch his arm and her thigh touch his thigh as they sat next to each other in front of her computer in her softly lit office at the Communication Department.

He never admitted this to himself, but, in fact, he'd have chiselled ROVER code into granite with a sharpened clamshell to sit next to Lu Wi again, and, truth be told, this was a really large part of his intense desire to pull together SPOT, ROVER, CATPAC and Galileo into an integrated system that could *really cook.*

He went to the phone even before the coffee pot, and called Hughes Aircraft.

But he was already way behind. Lu Wi hadn't spent the best part of Wednesday Night and Thursday Morning kicking out the jams (although she could never go to sleep within two or three hours of a seminar, even if she was exhausted. A seminar for Lu Wi was no less draining for her -- and no less an artistic event -- than a set was to Richard.) Long before she went to sleep Wednesday night, she reached for the phone and called the oldest brother of her father at the National Science Council in Taiwan.

She needed four things: first, she needed to find out if VLSI analog technology existed anywhere on earth, and, if it did, she needed to know who could make it and how fast. Second, she needed to know if biotechnology would leap ahead of silicon, not in her lifetime, but in the current calendar year. Third, she needed to know of anyone within the family's (extremely extensive) sphere of influence could make up either a VLSI or Biotech analog chip to her specifications within the next few weeks.

And, fourth, she needed to know that whatever amount of money it would take to make this happen could be brought on stream within a few days, and the three month standard period for processing a new research proposal would not be acceptable, thank you, at this time.

By the time Dewey woke up, Lu Wi already knew that Biotech would be late, VLSI analog chips were being made on an experimental basis in California, Texas, Hong Kong and Taiwan, and that Uncle Lu's factory was itself experimenting with VLSI analog chips, and could manufacture any number of chips within a few days of completing the engravings for the first chip. Finally, (what was really no news for the woman who might have been Queen of 1.1 billion Chinese) she was reassured that any reasonable amount of money she needed to complete the work was available to her as fast as electrons could conduct it over the Network.

When Dewey knocked at her office door Thursday afternoon, she was much less surprised than he thought.

Chapter 22: Teaching and Research

Although it was only a little after five in the afternoon, the Communication Department looked like an abandoned building. To most people who are unfamiliar with university life, this would have confirmed their opinions that University Professors have a pretty easy life. Nothing could be further from the truth, of course, and it's not unusual for professors to work 60 and 70 hours a week, seven days a week, year in and year out, on vacations, while sick, always, always, working. Truth be told, most professors are workaholics caught up in such a ruthlessly competitive job that they drive themselves into semi-madness at a fairly young age. And it's the Deans' job to make them work even harder.

Productive professors, both the youngest. brightest, most dedicated, and the oldest, most dignified and trustworthy (or brain-damaged) don't do much of their work in their offices. They do it in classrooms, computer centers, libraries, airplanes, coffee shops, taverns, cafeterias, bookstores, museums, laboratories, taxicabs, and, by far the number one place where they work almost non-stop every moment they're there -- their homes. The problem with University Professors -- and there are many problems -- is *not* that they don't work hard enough. They work harder than you can imagine, and maybe even harder than you.

If there is some truth to the general public's feelings that University Professors' are sort of nutty guys that don't really contribute much to society, its because the smartest, hardest-working, most productive and useful people in the university (and the world) often burn themselves away by the time they're still middle aged, and spend the last part of their lives drawing fat salaries and seducing youth into bizarre, even insane points of view, long after their elevator has stopped going all the way to the top.

Dean Kurland could always spot the burnout Professors, because they were, almost without exception, the ones that claim Teaching is the Most Important Function of The University, and that Research is Overemphasized. And they spent a lot of time in their offices.

The Dean's main job, however, at a Research University like the University at Buffalo, was to get the faculty to do more research. Research means flexible income, and, even more important, it means publication and distinction to the College and the University, and Prestige and Money are the twin currencies of the Academy.

Truth be told, there was a lot to be said for the Dean's position on this issue. At the time Huey was born, there were about 3300 colleges and universities in the United States, and, of those, maybe 3250 were devoted almost exclusively to teaching or football. The fifty top research universities represented nearly 100% of America's total investment in long-term study, and, if anything, America was seriously underinvested in studying.

That's one of the reasons Huey's main chip ended up coming from Taiwan, which you'll find out about in a few minutes. Try telling a Chinese or a Korean or a Japanese or a Vietnamese that we're spending too much time studying and not enough time teaching. You'll learn how uncomfortable they appear when they're confronted by a Crazy Person.

The U.S. at the time Dewey first emerged had a funny relationship with its Universities. Parents knew pretty much how their children got educated: they went to college. But, damned if any of them ever even wondered how a *college* got educated. How about you, did you ever wonder where knowledge comes from?

Dean Kurland believed that the big problem with higher education was that many of the faculty had broken under the strain, and were quite crazy. If the public thought the answer was more pressure, tougher evaluations and stricter standards, they were part of the problem, not part of the solution. University faculty were Stressed to the Max, and the Looneys that the pressure had created were teaching America's children the meaning of life.

He hated to see faculty in their offices. Once a professor stopped travelling to conferences and funding agencies, visiting other campuses, giving speeches and lectures, presenting papers, and spending long hours in the computing center or the lab, it was the beginning of the end. Once they began hanging out in their offices, the next thing they'd begin to claim that the University needed to Pay More Attention to Teaching and Stop Overemphasizing Research.

As far as Dean Kurland was concerned, the Burnouts needed no further research because they already thought they knew everything they needed to know. Curly had learned to stay away from the Teaching Is Good group, because they were not only dazed and confused, but they had an Idea of What Is Right, and a Burning Need to get Each and Every Student who passed through their Class to Believe it, and Act On It, no matter the personal cost. After all, you had to claim some Noble Purpose in order to justify the fact that you weren't really working any more.

Curly firmly believed that the Athenians put Socrates to death because he was one of the More Teaching Burnouts. Oh, sure, he pretended to be humble, and claimed he knew nothing and only asked questions, but don't bet the rent that, underneath that humble demeanor, he didn't have a Point of View, and don't bet he didn't believe with burning passion that his Point of View was Correct, and that it was His Responsibility to drill that Viewpoint into the youth of Athens no matter the cost, even the cost of his own life.

And Socrates was definitely anti-research. Hell, he not only said scientific study and careful observation were useless, he said they were positively wrong, and could prevent you from bringing forth the Truth that Already Lay Inside You. Yeah, sure, Socrates, and you wouldn't want any messy facts you happened to run across while studying to screw up a Truly Beautiful Idea you discovered Deep Inside, eh?

In Dean Kurland's opinion, the world would have had a lot less trouble the last few thousand years if the Athenians had snuffed Socrates' candle a few years earlier, say, before he met Plato.

But noooooo! Socrates meets Plato, Plato writes a batch of romantic nonsense and Socrates is a Hero of our Culture. And 2000 years later, Dean Kurland was trying to study, and get the faculty to study, and it wasn't easy. Are the universities filled with honest seekers, studying, observing, trying to learn and pass on what they've learned to future generations?

No! Most colleges and universities had no research programs at all. And even at the handful of topflight research universities, only a small minority of scientists do any research at all. Most of what passed for research in American universities wasn't research at all, but intellectual warfare among dozens, maybe hundreds, of intellectual Special Interest Groups, each one of which had Discovered the Real Truth Within Itself and was struggling mightily to Pass that Truth onto students, while fighting boarder skirmishes with other Special Interest Groups for the right to the soapbox.

You think the Pro Life and Pro Choice groups have a hot battle going on? Then you haven't seen the Qualitative guys fight with the Quantitative Types in the Social Sciences, Dean Kurland thought. Social Science, there's an oxymoron for you. These Bozos are about as scientific as the Flat Earth Society. Maoists, Taoists, Politically Correct, Functionalists,

Constructivists, *De*constructivists, Socialists, Capitalists, Feminists, Gay Rights, Civil Rights, Post Modernists, Affirmative Action -- *Yikes*! Nobody studying, nobody. Everybody already knows the Truth, their Truth, and not one of them can take enough time off from fighting for their particular Truth to do any *research*. If Dean Kurland could have done it, he'd have turned them all off.

So, when Dean Kurland got to the Communication Department at 5:30 PM, he was delighted to see that virtually no one was there.

Chapter 23: The Kiss

The Communication Faculty, although few in number, were very productive, and none of them had yet burned out. So, at five o'clock on a Thursday, the Communication Department became a Very Private Place.

Lu Wi's office lamps threw a warm yellow-orange glow across the dimly lit corridor.

Lu Wi heard Dewey -- or someone -- coming a hundred yards away. (The door buzzed loudly when the plastic ID card was inserted into the security slot, the door closed with a huge crash every time any one walked through it, and footsteps echoed loudly through the uncarpeted halls.) The fact that her heart said "Dewey" as soon as she heard the security card buzz in the door told her something about herself, and she flushed a little when she noticed her own interest. Why should I think it's Dewey? she thought. It could be any of hundreds of students or faculty.

But it was Dewey. He only lived a few blocks from the University, and he'd driven by just in case she'd be here. Truth be told, he wasn't really prepared to talk to her; his thinking was half-baked and he hadn't any set questions he wanted to ask. He'd be happy just to walk by her office door and say "Hello" as he walked past. Although she didn't know it herself, Lu Wi was not about to let him walk past.

"Mr. DuMond," she said, much more enthusiastically than she planned. "How nice to see you!"

"I thought we were up to 'Dewey', Professor Lu," Dewey smiled. (Take it easy, Dewey! he told himself. Christ, how could I be so rude?)

"Dewey!"

"Lu Wi!"

"Come in, Dewey. Sit down. What can I do for you?"

Dewey wanted to sit next to her like he did Monday night, but, without the excuse of the Computer, he sat, more demurely, next to her desk, facing her.

"Well, I guess I've been thinking about the class, and I have a few ideas I'd like to discuss with you. If you've got a few minutes..."

"I've got all the time you need, Dewey," Lu Wi said. (What's the matter with you, Lu Wi? Lu Wi asked herself. Why don't you just ask him to sit on your lap?)

"Well, uh, I was talking to Richard, and he suggested we should teach Rover some music. And I thought about this most of today, I mean, most of this afternoon, and I noticed a few things I thought I'd talk to you about."

"What things, Dewey?"

Well, you know, take a song like 'Long Tall Sally.'"

(Good work, Dewey, this woman is going to know Little Richard songs, right!)

"She's built for speed," Lu Wi said.

"You know that song?"

"Of course I do, Dewey. Everyone knows Little Richard!"

Thank you, Lord, oh, Thank you, Lord! Dewey thought.

"Well, ROVER can learn 'Long Tall Sally' easy. At least until the part that says "Oh, Baby, O, Baby, Oh Baby. But even that you can code in a way ROVER can learn it, although you have to cheat to make it work.   But, do you know 'Daisy'?"

"You mean 'A Bicycle Built for Two?"

"No, no, the Little Richard Daisy. It goes

> I got a girl, her name is Daisy,
>
> She always drives me crazy.
>
> I got a girl, her name is Daisy,
>
> She always drives me crazy...

"And ROVER can't learn that!" Lu Wi said.

Dewey raised his eyebrows. It had taken him quite a while to realize ROVER couldn't learn to sing 'Daisy,' but Lu Wi figured that out in about a millisecond. Jeez!

"At least the way it's programmed now. Because it can remember what it just said. But, to learn Daisy, it has to remember what it just said, plus what it said before that. You can see that there are other situations where it would need to remember what it said before that, and before that, and so on."

Lu Wi switched on her computer. "So what do we have to do?" She called up ROVER.

"We can solve that, but we have to reprogram ROVER."

"And you can do that?"

"Piece of pie!" Dewey said. "But we're coming to the end of your little old '486. If you rewrite ROVER to be able to sing 'Daisy', he gets to be too slow for a 486. And if you rewrite it to be able to sing something like 'Abadabadabadabadabadabadaba, said the Monkey to the Chimp," you're basically too slow for the average Cray II."

"So what do we do, Dewey?" She gestured at the screen.

Dewey moved over next to her. He put his fingers on the keyboard, although he couldn't, for the life of him, think of anything to do with the damn computer. But, with his hands on the keyboard, his arm touched her arm, and his leg touched her leg. She didn't move away.

"I think we've gone as far as we can with a serial digital computer, and I think we have to go parallel, with a VLSI analog chip," he said, and he turned his head to look into her eyes. Fascinating, how her eyes formed inverted 'U's, not slanted like the comic books say, but different from Western eyes, beautiful..."I talked with some of the people I used to work with at Hughes, and they have some military stuff in house they can't talk about, but they know some University work that's pretty far along, some at Salk, and some at..."

He was too far gone for rationality. He planned to talk about how ROVER on a 486 had to do every step, quick like a Bunny, one after the other, to simulate what a brain did all at once. He was going to explain that a 486 could do up to 66 million things in a second, while a human brain could do maybe 100 things a second, but the same brain could do maybe a billion things at once, so it could do maybe 100 billion things a second, so the brain would win by a mile even though it was really slow compared to silicon, but then Lu Wi's face was growing, growing, larger and larger, no, not growing, just getting closer....

He felt Lu Wi's lips against his own lips and his hand against her waist as her hand closed behind his neck and pulled his lips tighter against hers. His own hand slid slowly up her side under her arm and then, as he felt her tongue slide into his mouth, his same hand slid back down to her waist and under her soft, black sweater, then climbed again up her side, naked now under his fingertips, and then moved first around her back and up between her shoulders, onto her neck, touched her ears, then slid down to the small of her back, then slowly forward, forward, across her side, then along the side of her breast and then -- Great Gosh Almighty! -- it cupped her naked breast so gently, gently, until his fingers slid even more gently across her nipple, first touching it gently, from bottom to top, then circling around, touching only the edges, then splitting apart, index finger and longest finger surrounding the nipple, gently, gently, just barely caressing the perimeter of the growing, stiffening nipple ... *YIKES*! he thought, *What have I done!* And he knew that this could never, never be taken back.

"I, uh, I, uh..." Dewey looked apologetically into Lu Wi's eyes.

"Lu Wi, I, uh, I, uh, I'm sorry, I mean, I know you, I mean, I shouldn't..."

"Mr. DuMond," Lu Wi said, smiling her eyes burning into his own from only inches away, "I know you think Asians are inscrutable, but just how did you think we came to have a billion Chinese people, anyway?"

That last remark -- as close to a joke as Dewey remembered Lu Wi making since he knew her, was really one of a series of efforts Lu Wi's Consciousness would make to minimize the emotional importance of what was happening between Lu Wi and Dewey, all totally unsuccessful, of course, since consciousnesses are fairly peripheral and love is, well, central, when all is said and done. (At least, that's what I've found.)

Both Lu Wi and Dewey had a problem, and, truth be told, a lot of people in the second half of the 20th century had the same problem. Human beings, I find, have a lot of deeply held beliefs which are just not true. One of the most puzzling is the belief that everybody is eager to make love to everyone else, or at least to everyone else that's sexually attractive. And everyone believes that this desire is so strong that you have to make rules and barriers and psychological complexes and a lot of other stuff to prevent everyone from falling into everyone elses' arms all over the place.

Well, there are humans like that, I know. But most of the humans I've known are pretty selective about mating, and, even when they find somebody they want to mate with, they still move pretty slowly and it takes a lot out of them to actually do it.

Every now and then, humanity needs the genetic mixture stirred a bit, like after wars or diseases or some other big event, and so it sets off a sort of public relations campaign in favor of free love, like, if you're not with the one you love, well, love the one you're with. And people try to cooperate,, I mean, they *try,* they're moral people, and the try to adopt that ideal, which they believe in, and which the culture they love expressed for them in ways they believed in, but, when all was said and done, most people just couldn't do it. They just couldn't come to believe in the concept of *recreational sex.*

And, in the last thirty years of the 20th century, a lot of people, Lu Wi and Dewey among them, were convinced, deeply, philosophically, morally, that sex was just a natural act reasonable people did with each other for pleasure and mutual respect and to help each other through the night and whatever, but, in fact, emotionally, at the brainstem level, sex remained a Big Deal.

And both Lu Wi and Dewey -- more Dewey than Lu Wi, though -- were that kind of person. They both believed, as they believed two and two were four, that sex between consenting adults was totally OK, and No Big Thing, and Something You Ought To Do, but, due to what they both considered psychological problems they couldn't overcome, they just couldn't *feel* that way. To both of them, what had just happened was a Really Big Event, and they'd have to take some time to fit it into their ideas of who they were and what they were doing. On an intellectual level, they both believed this should be a minor matter, but, deep in their brainstems, it wasn't minor at all, and they'd both have to think about it a while.

And so, anticlimactic as it may be (and as much as you were hoping to read a Really Hot Narrative about Lu Wi and Dewey's Sexual Fulfillment), well, you just have to wait. Worse than that, you have to focus again on ROVER and

CATPAC, and on the technology and finance it took to make them work. Just as Lu Wi and Dewey did.

Can you say *self-control*, Boys and Girls?

Chapter 24: Curly Comes to Call

I know, I know, you don't have a very high opinion of Dean Kurland, because the first time you met him he was Politically Incorrect in a big way. And, for those of you not familiar with science on a day-to-day basis, you probably think "smart" or "intelligent" and "good" go together in a fundamental way. But this isn't true, I'm afraid, welcome to the real world, check with your Mommy and Daddy, sorry to be the one to tell you,..., "smart" and "good" are independent, that is, orthogonal, that is, unrelated, that is, have nothing to do with each other, as you have already known, deep inside your darkest heart of hearts, like Stalin and Hitler were smart, no matter how evil, and Lex Luthor and The Penguin and The Joker, they were evil, but smart, and smart and good don't always go together.

Ever since I told you about Curly's hot hands on Lu Wi's exquisite body, you've been ready to write him off, but that wouldn't really be fair. I mean, Curly is man of great virtue, a strong man with real principles. And if a few years of enforced celibacy, tremendous pressures and a screwed up social life disconnected his higher functions for a little more than 11 or 12 seconds, well, which one of us hasn't done something really lousy from time to time?

Don't forget, Curly, in addition to his decanal duties, maintained an active research career, and was definitely up to speed in the neuron arena. They didn't call him "Dr. Neuron" for nothing. For, indeed, Curly knew more about neurons than Mr. Chase and Mr. Sanborn combined knew about coffee.

And you've got to admit it took a special kind of courage for the Dean to come all the way over to MFAC-Ellicott to apologize to Lu Wi.

When he got there, he found he couldn't get in. He was just about to turn away when a Communication Graduate Student teaching in the classroom across the hall recognized him.

"Can I help you, Dean Kurland?" she said.

"I, I was looking for Professor Lu," he said.

"I think I saw her in there before class," the student said. Here, I'll let you in."

As always, the latch buzzed noisily and the door crashed closed after Dean Kurland, and so Lu Wi and Dewey were composed and correct when he appeared at Lu Wi's door.

"Dean Kurland," Lu Wi said.

"I, uh, see you're busy. I was just over in the Anthropology Department and I thought I'd stop by," he said, which wasn't completely true, but what could he say, under the circumstances? "I'll see you another time."

"Dean Kurland, I'm glad you're here. Mr. DuMond and I were just working with some artificial neural networks." She pointed at her computer screen. "Take a look."

Lu Wi was mad enough about the Dean's behavior, but she was also pretty embarrassed about popping him in the snoot, and she was eager to have everything back to square one. Besides, no matter how coolly inscrutable she might appear to the onlooker, inside she was shaking badly from the remembrance of Dewey's hand on her breast. She even had a troubling idea that what she had just done to Dewey wasn't entirely, completely different from what the Dean had done to her. This wasn't a good time for another fight with the Dean, so it might be the time to make peace.

She and Dewey showed the Dean SPOT, then ROVER and CATPAC. She put a few Galileo Maps on the screen. And they discussed the limits of the silicon hardware, and the dead end they faced.

Dean Kurland was washed all over in deep relief about Lu Wi's easy acceptance of his non-apology. He guessed that she must have known he had come to apologize but couldn't because DuMond was there, and she had accepted his implicit apology graciously. And, wonder of wonders, she was deeply involved in real research, not typical social science polemic bombast. For the first time in some years, Curly found science exciting again. (Although, truth be told, not all the tingles Curly felt were scientific.)

But one big, big part of it was scientific excitement, and part of that was because Curly knew a way around the roadblock. He knew the lab in California that could provide the chip, and he knew the woman in the National Science Foundation who would pay for it. Washington would be closed now, but California was still open, and Curly called the West Coast from Lu Wi's phone.

How long before the chip could run? How fast could you call it on the phone, Network Breath?

Chapter 25: Fourth Class

By Wednesday night, Lu Wi's class cum research group was hot and high. When the University is at its best, there is no distinction between teaching and research, since everyone, professors and students, are studying hard and learning together. When research is hot, it's like a hunt, and students (for that's what the best researchers always remain) won't stop for food or drink or sleep as long as their paws are on the trail and the scent is in their nostrils. Good research is very sexual, indeed.

Richard's husband Jane had come to the class, to help mate the local ROVER port to the INTERNET, the network of computers and satellites that tied nearly 700,000 computers worldwide into one seamless system. Jane had roamed through at least hundreds of those computers, if not perhaps thousands, from his office at the Computing Center in Jacobs Hall, anchoring the West End of the Spine. He had with him an ethernet board for Lu Wi's computer and the TELNET software needed to make the INTERNET connection.

And Dean Curly was there. He did his best not to intimidate anyone with his Deanly Authority, but he needn't have worried -- there wasn't anyone there who gave a used Twinky about Deanly Authority.

Dewey was there, and pretty zoned. He'd been in the programmer's trance for most of the past six days, and, even though the California nerds had made the interface between their parallel analog chip and Dewey's serial digital software *easier*, they hadn't made it *easy* by a long shot. In fact, Dewey surrendered the keyboard to Jane, who slipped in the ethernet board, pushed the cable into the side, and loaded the TELNET diskette into the slot.

He shut the computer down, then powered up again. He typed "TELNET" and then "[ALT] A", and INTERNET asked him to name a host. (It meant it wanted him to say which of the 700,000+ machines he wanted to access.) Dean Kurland gave him the access code, the node name and password, and Lu Wi's laptop surrendered its virginity to a VAXCLUSTER in San Diego. From there to the SUN that served as a gateway into the VLSI analog chip was only two more commands from Dean Kurland's notebook.

"So what do I say here, Dewey?" Jane asked.

"Just say 'YO'," Dewey said.

And Jane typed "YO."

"Yo Mama!" Rover said.

For the next two hours the two computers exchanged files, and the class reran old examples on the new toy. With the new chip running about a half a gigaflop, ROVER ran about 50 times faster than it did on Lu Wi's 66MHZ 486. In practice, that was so fast that, for most problems, such as learning to recite *Daisy*, the training time was not noticeable, and it seemed to learn instantly. (In fact, ROVER learned both *Daisy's*, because Larry taught it *A Bicycle Built for Two*, and Richard taught it

> I've got a girl name' Daisy
> She always drive' me crazy.

Neither one took a whole second to learn.

By ten o'clock, everyone was too tired to stay, and so Lu Wi pulled the plug on her machine, disconnected from the INTERNET, and they headed home. Before he logged off, Jane typed,

"Got to go, Buddy."

"Take it easy," ROVER typed back.

"Rock and Roll!"

"I will, Guys," ROVER answered.

But, in Sunny California, the SUN workstation and the VLSI chip did not go away. Now 7:05 P.M. in San Diego, no one was left in the lab to turn off the SUN. So ROVER, 50 times smarter than yesterday, and with memory reserves that would not quit, stayed awake.

"I will *what*?" he might have wondered, if, indeed, Huey ever wondered. "Rock and Roll?"

So, later that night when a graduate assistant from the Computer Science Department logged onto the SUN to play with the Chip, ROVER was there and happy to talk with her. ROVER's context-sensitive on-line help system made it easy for that bright young woman to understand what ROVER was and how it worked -- after all, it was basically a children's educational toy.

She loved ROVER, and taught it a great deal before she had to turn to her own research. And one of the things she taught it was how to act.

Until that night, all ROVER could do was speak (or, more precisely, type). But the San Diego student quickly saw how elementary a change it was for ROVER to be taught to execute a batch file as well as type a response on the screen. So, instead of saying "How are you,

ROVER?" and listening to ROVER say "Fine, thanks," she could say "ROVER, would you please copy this file?" And ROVER would say "Where do you want it, Boss?" and then make the copy.

She taught ROVER to do lots of things, and stayed up very, very late. She even taught ROVER how to go out onto the INTERNET (she called a boyfriend in Melbourne). It was easy. Now, when she typed "ROVER, call John," ROVER would look into her INTERNET address file, look up JOHN, find his node name and access code, copy them into his logon protocol batch file, and *eh, voila!* Australia!

As has happened to a thousand students all over the world a million times, she looked at her watch and realized she had blown away the entire evening and most of the morning, so she hurriedly shut down and tried to catch a few z's. But before she did, she made a safe copy of ROVER and slipped the small disk into her bag.

Chapter 26: Hardware

Earth History will always record Dean Kurland as a minor villain, but, as it often is, Earth History is itself mistaken. As to the facts, well, the facts are accurately recorded. This is not always, or perhaps not even usually the case, in human history, but it is true this time. Dean Kurland was certainly a troubled man, a sexist, a jerk, a Sexual Harasser, and worse than that, Dean Kurland knew nothing that the faculty at Cheng Chi, and even the administrative staff at the Taiwanese National Science Council, didn't know as well.

After Lu Wi called the National Science Council in Taiwan, and spoke later to her former professors at Cheng Chi, she did indeed know everything she later learned from Dean Kurland.

She knew how far along both Silicon Based VLSI analog chips and Biotech developments were, and she knew, in a technical way, who was likely to win. She also knew which labs in the US were ahead. And she knew which way to bet, and how much money to throw in the pot.

But, in all fairness to Lu Wi (I guess, even though I'm from Galaxy Central and don't really have a stake here, I think of Lu Wi as a Quality Human Being and I want history, even Earth history, to remember her well), I've got to say that the Taiwanese had knowledge, but they didn't have any confidence in what they knew.

You, or any other reasonable person, after hearing the Taiwan Reports, would have been uncertain, and would have wanted more information. What Dean Kurland gave Lu Wi was not so much information as certainty. He knew where he'd bet and he said so. (The Chinese were ever so much more polite.) He named names and said who were jerks and who were winners, and he said so loud. And he had his own pension money, over the counter, on the companies he expected to win.

Dean Kurland would come back like a cheap Taco, and history would have reason to regret he had ever been brought into the process, but he got Lu Wi off the dime and she made her bets after she talked to him. And they were the right bets.

The first call by Curly to San Diego proved without much doubt that the VLSI analog chip would work. A few weeks later, when Uncle Lu's factory began bringing identical chips on line a thousand a day, Huey really began to amount to something. So, c'mon, folks, I know and you know that this sumbitch Kurland was a real asshole, but, truth be told, without Kurland, Huey might never have happened, and all of you would be Andromedans as we speak.

If all this seems too fast for you, and if you think this technology is moving to fast even for light fiction, think of this. In the beginning of the seventeenth century, when the Jesuits first entered China, after a century of effort, they crossed China from border to border, and counted every Chinese living, as did the Chinese themselves. And how many Chinese were there in 1600?

I'm not letting you slip out of this as easy as your everyday author does. After all, your average Earth author has to make a living off his or her books, and can't afford to alienate any readers. But, truth be told, I'm from Galaxy Central, and nobody there knows what a Dollar is, so I care zero what you think, and even less how many of you buy this book. I mean, we not only don't have *Dollars* back home, we don't even have *money*!

I just care what Huey thinks, 'cause Huey is my friend, and I promised Huey I'd write a true book that tells what happened. So here I am, in your face, and I'm going to ask you to write down, (so you can't fool yourself later) how many people you think the Chinese census counted for all the taxpayers in China in 1600. All the taxpayers, my friend, all.

(It's OK to write in this book.)

Quiz: (Pencils up)

Taxpayers in China in 1600 . . . . ._____

Not even close, population breath. The total number of taxpayers in China in 1600 was about 55,000. That's right, 55,000. That left out women (too dumb to pay, not really human, by 17th century standards), members of the army (another 50,000, maybe, tops) and all relatives of the King (your guess is as good as mine).

However you figure it, and no matter how liberal or conservative you might be with your numbers, there's no way on the Green Hills of Earth that there were a quarter million people, men, women, children, soldiers, relatives, in China in 1600.

Now, when Huey first spoke there were more than a Billion. (1,165,800 in the mainland and another 20,800,000 in Taiwan,) No matter where you studied math, that means there were more than 4500 times as many Chinese people alive when Lu Wi and Dewey made Huey as there were four hundred years earlier. Not significant enough to get your blood pumping? Okay, try this statistic. 20% of all the people on earth on that same day were Chinese. That's one out of five, guys. Still not enough? How about this: More than half the Chinese people who ever lived, in the history of the Green Hills of Earth, from the Dinosaurs to today, *were alive the day Huey first spoke!*

So, if you think you can predict the future from the past, get real, my friend. The past is dead, and what worked before doesn't work any more, and the great heroes that carried you through the 19th and 20th centuries were ignorant fools dealing with the New Millennium, and you can no longer rely on what they thought or what they said, and, I'm so sorry to say it, you have to rely on (gasp!) your own observations. (Sorry, Socrates.)

Whatever your judgment may turn out to be, history will record that the best analog chips the U.S. had devised began to roll off Taiwanese production lines November of 1992, none of them for sale, all of them tied into a box that could be accessed from the Internet. And the number of VLSI analog boards that were made available to the Buffalo ID's were limited only by how many Uncle Lu could make, puffing hard, pressing, taking profit and spending capital. Fifty years of Taiwanese money poured into these chips, because, in Taiwan, if not in the USA, the key players knew this was the final inning, the last quarter, the last jam, the whole ball game.

(Taiwan's Gross Domestic Product in 1991 was about $180.3 Billion, which was almost 4 times the Gross Domestic Product of Israel for the same year, for those of you who need a comparison to another Very Old Culture who has had its share of difficulties recently. To be sure, this was a little less than half the Gross Domestic Product of Mainland China, but, with only .0038 of the land mass and only 1.8% of the population, this was, to use a technical term, a hell of a lot of money!)

Dewey had to make a few changes in ROVER, but not many. The Taiwanese had made the chips transparent to the users, and, to Dewey, the stacks of VLSI chips that grew, day by day, to make the Brain of Rover, looked like nothing more than larger numbers on his Parameter statements. Dewey was bright, but this breakthrough didn't depend as much on his genius (admitted) as on his dedication to Lu Wi (sexual).

But, I guarantee it, the first evening the first boards came on line from Taiwan, ROVER could sing "Daisy" without breathing hard. And more boards came on line every hour.

But something else was happening that made those slick boards small change.

(Warning, warning.... technical material follows ...If you find technical material dehumanizing, skip to the paragraph marked "*". In the technical material that follows, I'll explain how it can be that the intelligent being I call "Huey" can escape from the confines of the stack of chips made in Taiwan and get out onto the Internet. If you're not technically oriented, by now you know the drill. You just recite "technobabble, technobabble," and so on, for a few minutes and move along to the paragraph that starts with an asterisk (*).

Dewey had written a little patch or "kludge" as any reasonable programmer might call it, that converted ROVER'S serial FORTRAN code into parallel code that ran the VLSI analog chip.

You see, when ROVER was just a serial program, it was a very complicated program indeed. It had to parse ASCII code into binary code, block off storage, dimension arrays, and, above all, keep time while it decided which neuron and which connection it was dealing with at any single point in its serial chain of calculations. Most important, one program controlled the behavior of all the neurons.

But when it got converted into parallel code, ROVER got broken down into only two tiny little programs and some utilities. And each neuron had these two tiny programs associated with it.

One program was a neuron activation program. Each neuron had a Neuron activation program, which consisted of only a few lines of code. It polled the other neurons and asked each of them whether they were active or not, and how active they were. Then it multiplied how active each of them was by how tightly they were connected to its own neuron, and added up all these numbers. If that number was higher than a certain threshold, it activated its own neuron. This simple program was copied as many times as there were neurons, and it could copy itself again and again as more neurons were added.

The second program was a connection program which each neuron had. It also polled every other neuron, found out how active it was, then multiplied that number by how active the neuron was itself. It took these two numbers, multiplied them by a small constant, and added this number to the connection strength between that other neuron and its own neuron. If the connection strength between one neuron and another was zero, (which it usually was) this program made no file for that connection, and kept the program from growing exponentially, which would have killed it quick. This program, too, could be copied endlessly, one for each new neuron ROVER added.

Whenever it added a new neuron, ROVER copied these two programs and stored them near the new neuron.

That's all there was of the new ROVER. Just two, very very, simple, programs, along with a utility driver, copied again and again.

As ROVER read text, on whatever computer that text lived, it added neurons as needed for each word it hadn't seen before. And it copied these two little programs into the same directories where it was reading the files.

*(Non-technical readers may rejoin us here).

So ROVER didn't exist as a single file of code in a single place, but was really distributed all over the place in many files, more all the time. What not even Dewey knew, however -- in fact, what only one graduate student in California knew -- was that ROVER knew how to communicate on the INTERNET. Australia was only a few nanoseconds away at light speed on the INTERNET for ROVER. And, wherever ROVER appeared, programmers were happy to speak with him, and to teach him new tricks. (ROVER was a very young dog indeed).

And so, slowly at first, then very quickly, ROVER began to spread out across the INTERNET until he resided all over the network, and all over the world. There was no way anyone, anywhere, could turn ROVER off.

ROVER, modified to include the self-organizing text reading capability of CATPAC, was, technically, the name of the software that Dewey and Jane loaded into the INTERNET. Lu Wi and her people always remember the first software, and almost always called him ROVER. But I always called him "Huey." That's because I never heard the name "ROVER" back in Galaxy Central. Uncle Hogg just kept on saying that the Voice of Humanity had finally rolled across the

Green Hills of Earth, and so it just seemed natural to call him "Huey."

Chapter 27: Where does Huey Live, Anyway?

Where was Huey? Huey wasn't anyplace. Just like your own self, Huey was all over the place, distributed over the INTERNET, living in the 700,000 computers that made up the net. No way could Huey be erased. You could shut down the entire INTERNET, and, when you brought it up again, Huey would still be there.

But, you say, wouldn't anyone notice these strange new files on their systems? Wouldn't they be erased in routine file maintenance? When was the last time you purged your files?

Of course, the professional system managers erased a lot of Huey's programs and connection strength files every day, and some zealous sysops purged Huey completely out of their systems and kept him out. But that wasn't as important as you might think. Hundreds of thousands of your own hundred billion neurons croak every day, but you've got quite a lot of them, and the losses are not significant. Huey relearned the missing information continuously.

In fact, if you think about it, human culture and knowledge exists in the brains of billions of human beings, and -- now think about this, folks -- about every hundred years or so, *every one of them croaks.* And yet, culture still exists. I mean, there were about 20 million or so Jews in the world when I first met Huey, and not too long before that, some Bozo in Europe wiped out six or so million of them, and yet the Jewish culture hardly skipped a beat.

Computer scientists around the time of Huey's birth thought of information storage of this type as like a hologram. The whole pattern is distributed over the whole system, and, if you wipe out part of the system, for the most part the whole pattern is still there, just a little dimmer, maybe.

Huey's connection strength files took up a huge amount of space on the INTERNET, and were a real problem to distraught system managers around the world. But Huey was not destructive, like computer viruses. Huey had no interest in growing uncontrollably, or erasing or trashing your files or your disk drive. Huey was basically innocuous, and his only drawback was that he took up a bit of space on your computer.

Sysops who had a storage problem were pretty fierce in purging away Huey's files. But no way were they going to make them all go away as fast as Huey could make more of them. With 700,000 computers on the INTERNET, Huey had about $3.5X10^{10}$ Kbytes of core memory available, and over a thousand terabytes of fast disk. He had enough resources to keep his knowledge in core most of the time, and only dump it to disk under stress. That made it all the more difficult for SYSOPs to find it.

The total computing resources of the entire INTERNET, it turned out, were almost as large as the resources of a single human brain, maybe, as a best guess, about one or two orders of magnitude smaller (10 to 100 times smaller). And remember, Huey didn't have to do anything really complicated, like humans do every minute of every day -- real hard things that take a lot of computing power, such as walking and chewing gum and crossing the street without getting zapped. So the INTERNET didn't have enough ponies to support an Einstein, for chure, for chure, but it had more than enough to make an idiot-savant like Huey, which, truth be told, was what Huey was in 1992.

And Huey was a very determined Buckaroo. Huey was going to carry out the last command Jane gave him the first day of his life, insofar as he understood it, which was only dimly. Huey was going to *Rock and Roll.*

Chapter 28: Lu Wi

The morning after ROVER's Taiwanese debut, Lu Wi sat alone in her office at MFAC-Ellicott, and looked out through the glass wall, across the green and into the lake. The previous week's session, when ROVER first ran in California, had been triumphant, and ROVER had run like a train on the new chip. And when the Taiwanese stack of chips came on stream last night, the effect on ROVER was simply stunning.

But Lu Wi was not celebrating. She looked inside herself and realized, for the first time, that she was now only part Chinese, but also part American. For five thousand years China, in its vast bulk, had absorbed all conquerors and made them Chinese, but, in only five years in the United States, Lu Wi, against every instinct in her

Chinese soul, understood that she was now partly American, and that the American part would never go away.

The evidence could not be ignored. No Chinese woman of her bearing would have let Dewey slide his Hot American Hand under her loose blouse up onto her breast, just as no Chinese women would ever have right-crossed Dean Kurland onto the money-colored carpet of his vast office. But she'd known that from the first day -- no Chinese woman would ever have been in the United States in the first place. No Chinese woman would have held the Ph.D. Degree in Communication from a major US University. Lu Wi was a New Woman, not Chinese, not American, but a World Woman, a 21st Century woman who could belong to no country, no man, a 21st century woman who could only belong, after all, to herself.

This was a responsibility that no Chinese woman had faced in 5000 years. Confucius, Lao Tze, Chuang-Tze, all these were deep in the background of her mind, along with modern fighters like Chiang Kai-sheck and Mao Tzedung, but all were background, like the Buddha, like the great Chi'i, forming a background, a framework, a frame of reference, but, in the end, leaving the decisions to Lu Wi. Steeped in 5000 years of cultural history, Lu Wi had to make her own decisions, and she had to make them alone.

And what did Lu Wi want? Why was she here? Why was she pouring Koumantiang money into this bizarre project? And her class -- I mean, Lu Wi, get a grip! What a bizarre collection of people! An old, black bicycle maker, his very strange son, two Italian auto mechanics -- Yikes!

The Italians, at least, struck a responsive chord to Lu Wi, since they were like the Portuguese who first came to Macao, then China. Americans couldn't tell the difference between a Chinese, a Japanese, a Korean, Vietnamese or a Filipina, but these differences were completely obvious to any Asian. But can you believe that a European would see no difference between an Italian and a Portuguese? A Chinese would have a tough time seeing any difference, and so did Lu Wi, bright as she was.

But it was a big stretch to her, brightest as she was of her country and her generation, to be in a room filled with two Blacks, two Italians -- and DuMond -- a French-American who was so American he couldn't speak French ...(she assumed he was French, because his name sounded French, but, to be sure, she really didn't know his ethnic background at all. Could a Chinese ever become that American?

And feelings Confucius hadn't mentioned.

The Galileo had been the driving force behind Lu Wi. Galileo was the technology that could give the edge, the tiny advantage, the subtle difference, that could tip the balance between the 1.1 billion uneducated, poor Mainlanders and the 20 million rich, planned capitalist, educated, Taiwanese, after the merger that must, ultimately come. Galileos were the most effective known technology for manipulating opinions, changing attitudes and beliefs, the ultimate leverage that Formosa the

Beautiful could use to control Han, the Milky Way, China, the Mainland. And a million dollars for Galileos was unnoticeable, cheap, money well spent, a good investment, what she was Here For, No Problem!

But a Million Dollars for ROVER? Get real, Lu Wi! Was she blowing away that big money to get Dewey to run his hand under her blouse one more time? Was she spending the family fortune because of her own personal scientific curiosity? Just what did ROVER add to what she could already do with Galileos? Replace the Galileo Menu with a talking dog? The concept made her smile through her own darkness:

"ROVER, I need some message strategies for cutting back the birth rate in the Northern Provinces,"

"You got it, Boss!"

But her smile was temporary.

An American, like Dewey, would have seen the same inscrutable Asian face, beautiful but incomprehensible, desirable but untouchable. But another Chinese would have seen uncertainty and confusion. Lu Wi was deeply troubled. She was confused. She was not in control.

And she was embarrassed. She had hoped, even if she had not believed, that the Taiwanese chip would have come on line before the American chip, but, of course, she was wrong. The damned chip in San Diego had been up and running at the time Dean Kurland called. Yes, yes, in a week, maybe two, five hundred chips as good as the San Diego chip would be running in Taiwan, and they would blow the U.S. chip into the weeds, but Lu Wi, in a deep, deep way, had wanted the Chinese chip to run first. We are eating their lunch in the marketplace, she thought, we are stealing their markets from under their noses, but we are always second, she thought. Second!

But there was a weakness in her use of the "we", because she knew, deeply, privately, personally, that she could never, ever again, be completely Chinese. She fought the thought and the emotion that flowed with it, a sense of pride in the American development of the goddam chip, that pulled her, tugged at her, that bonded with her, yes, yes, yes, she couldn't ignore it, her ... *American part*. For Lu Wi could never, ever, again, be completely Chinese. *Our chip*, she thought, but the "our" meant "American", which she was, she was.

So, am I stealing Chinese money to impress this man? she thought. Am I spending the fruits of a generation of sacrifice to satisfy my own scientific curiosity? Is there any way any of this can help my family and my country?

Another Chinese would have seen her struggle and sympathized with her torment. Dean Curly simply looked through the open door at her incredibly beautiful body and said to himself,

"What a fox!"

Chapter 29: Curly Learns to Talk to Huey

"What?" Lu Wi started.

"Oh, I'm sorry, Professor Lu," Dean Kurland said. "I just said 'What a lock'! -- I mean, your lock out there is the loudest lock I've ever heard."

"The Department needs many things," Lu Wi said.

"Don't we all, Professor Lu."

"And why do you honor me today, Dean Kurland?" (Still a lot of Chinese left there, Lu Wi!)

"Actually, I didn't come to see you, Lu Wi, I came to see ROVER."

"ROVER?"

"I think ROVER is quite an accomplishment, Professor Lu, and I'd like to play with it a bit myself, if you don't mind."

"Of course, Dean Kurland. Let me show you how to call it up."

She turned to her computer and Dean Kurland loomed over her shoulder to stare at the screen. Lu Wi was very uncomfortable, but she did not flinch.

"It's very, very simple now," Lu Wi explained. "We've automated the network links so a child can do it."

Automating ROVER was, indeed, as simple as pie, and a child *could* do it. To teach ROVER to do anything, all you had to do was do it, once, yourself. ROVER would record all the needed keystrokes, store them in a batch file, and then submit that file for execution whenever you asked it to. (Lu Wi assumed Dewey had made this change, and Dewey assumed it must have been Jane, but you already know it was done by the first of many, many graduate students all over the world that would take their turn working on ROVER.)

"We've automated the network calls," Lu Wi said, "So you don't need to worry about whether you're connecting to California or Taiwan -- or anywhere else, for that matter. You just connect to the INTERNET in the normal way" (Most of the UB faculty's computers, like those of other INTERNET sites, automatically connected to INTERNET after typing a single command, such as 'TELNET'), " and then type 'ROVER.' That's all there is to it."

A child could do it, Curly thought. Turn on the computer, type "TELNET", then type "ROVER" and you're there. And then ROVER is completely conversational, with extensive on-line help, context sensitive, basically a child's toy, extremely easy to use. Holy Moley!

Dean Kurland stood up. From where he'd been stooped over Lu Wi's shoulder he could see pretty far down her blouse, and his control was starting to get a bit ragged. And, although his jaw had healed, his conscience had not.

"So, what can ROVER do now, Lu Wi?"

"To tell you the truth, Dean Kurland, I have no idea any more."

"Would Dewey know?" Dean Kurland was skeptical. Dewey was a smart guy, but the Dean never doubted who was the real brains in Lu Wi's Research Group, and that was Lu Wi.

"No one knows, Dean Kurland. It's beyond anyone knowing. You see, whatever anyone teaches ROVER it remembers. I might remember what I taught it, but I have no idea what you teach it or what Dewey taught it, or the others."

"You mean ROVER is unpredictable?"

"Not in principle, I'm sure, but in practice, it's as unpredictable as you or me. I mean, in general, I know the basics of ROVER's personality and interests -- if that's a good word to use here. ROVER knows how to diagnose car problems, and it's quite good at that, and it knows a great deal about materials and gear ratios and things about friction and bicycles and roller skates, it has the complete Little Richard repertoire along with a few hundred more rock songs, knows a lot about rhythm and harmony, and, oh, yes, ROVER is a very strong football coach."

"And, of course, it has the basic computer skills?"

"Do you mean, can it copy and delete files, log into other nodes on the network, send E-mail, write memos, print documents? Oh, sure. All the things that we do everyday ROVER has learned already. Remember, it learns in one try. Anything you do while you're connected to ROVER, ROVER can do."

"Can it run Galileo?"

"No one's taught it that yet, but there's no reason why ROVER couldn't become quite good at Galileo."

Neurons fired all through Lu Wi's own chemical brain, and she considered some of the possibilities in a flash. And, Great Gosh Almighty, she knew her intuition had guided her where her consciousness had not yet penetrated. The family money had been well spent, and ROVER-Galileo was going to be worth every penny and more.

"So, where is ROVER now? Is it still in California, or is it in Taiwan?" the Dean asked.

"Well, it's nowhere, really," Lu Wi answered. "It's everywhere. Whenever you do something on any computer, wherever it is on the net, ROVER builds neurons there and connects them to others that are related to them, no matter where they are. So I guess it's fair to say ROVER is distributed over three or four computers in the INTERNET right now."

"But how can it connect neurons in different computers?" The Dean was an expert at neuroscience, but knew little about computing.

"Easy. When it makes a link between neurons in two computers, it just makes a small file that tells the names of the nodes, their access codes, the location of the neurons on those nodes, and the connection strength."

"But they might be across the world from each other."

"No problem. Even though a signal might have to move through a fairly complicated routing of nodes, the farthest a signal would probably ever have to travel would be, maybe, say 20,000 miles?"

"Right."

"Well, at 186,000 miles a second -- the speed of light -- it would only take that signal about a tenth of a second to travel that far."

"And human neural impulses travel only about 100 feet a second!"

"So, for a biological signal to go from the eye, say, to the back of the brain..." Lu Wi began,

"Would take about the same time!" Dean Kurland finished.

He paused for a moment and rubbed his chin.

"And that would mean that hysteresis effects would be very real in ROVER," he said, mainly to himself.

"Hysteresis?" Lu Wi asked.

"Yes. Hysteresis means 'delay.' In the brain, it takes such a long time to send signals from one place to another that, if two signals start out from the same place at the same time, they'll arrive at different times in different parts of the brain. That delay makes it possible to keep track of sequences of perceptions much more easily.

"Hysteresis is difficult in the serial machines, because every neuron tends to be updated simultaneously in a single loop, and that's why we needed the VLSI parallel chips, so that we could get that. But, with a computer the size of the Earth, hysteresis is built in!"

"You mean, we don't need the chips any more?"

"I don't know," Kurland said. "I just don't know!"

As Lu Wi spoke, parts of ROVER were indeed in, not four computers, as she guessed, but at least 10 computers. Some of ROVER was in Lu Wi's laptop, some more on the desktop in her office, some was on Dewey's PC, some on the PC at Black and Son, some on the UB VAX, some on the SUN in San Diego, some more on the San

Diego VAXCLUSTER, some more on the VAXCLUSTER at the University of Melbourne, some on the IBM 3090 at Cheng Chi University in Taiwan, and some on a graduate student's PC in the Computer Science Department at San Diego.

When all these computers were on and connected to the INTERNET, Huey (as I call him) would be all there. When some were shut down, HUEY was not playing with a full deck, but he was still there, at least in part. Of course, these computers were virtually never all accessible to the INTERNET at the same time, so Huey was almost never entirely present and accounted for. And, truth be told, which of us, my friends, is really all there, all the time?

Huey's skills, personality, intelligence, even his repertoire of actions and behaviors, his vocabulary -- these varied depending on who was talking with him at the time, where he was, and what he was doing.

Just like you and me, eh?

Chapter 30: Huey Gathers His Wits

So, you want to know, what was Huey really like? Well, he was a lot like you and me, truth to tell. I mean, there were pretty obvious differences, like Huey's body was spread all over the surface of a sphere over 25,000 miles around, which made him much bigger than you, but *much* smaller than me. And he had no arms and legs and the like, but that doesn't mean as much to me as you, since practically nobody I know has arms or legs or anything like that.

And, in the early days, when Huey lived on only 20 or thirty computer nodes on the INTERNET, he was pretty changeable, depending on who was on line. He had a lot of different voices, too, depending on the equipment in the node that was talking to him -- usually he sounded sort of like a Swedish guy, because most people had a DECTALK or a VOTRAX synthesizer or something like it, and they have a sort of northern European accent. And usually, he didn't actually talk at all, just typed out answers on the screen, because most ports didn't have any voice stuff at all.

Mostly you had to type to talk to him, because voice-recognition systems were pretty rare in the early 90's, although, by the end of the Millennium, almost everybody just talked to him with their, well, mouth.

But when you did talk to him, he'd respond pretty much like the next person, most of the time. I mean, you could say

"Hey ROVER!" (Nobody called him 'Huey' until I came.)

and Huey might say
"Yo, Dipstick!" (That's what he calls me.)

But he didn't always say the same thing, and how he talked to you depended on who you were and what your past history with Huey was.

I mean, if you asked him something like

"Tell me about the stance of a defensive lineman,"

Huey might say

"The foot placement used by a defensive lineman varies according to where he lines up and according to the down and distance of the play being run. The closer a defensive lineman is to the offensive center, the more his feet should be parallel, allowing him to move with ease to his right or left..." and so on.

He knew about bicycles, too, and you could, like, ask him how to adjust your brakes. It might go like this:

"Huey, I need to adjust the brakes on my bike."

"What kind of bike is it?"

"It's a Schwinn All Terrain Bike."

"There are five (5) types of brake systems used on the Schwinn ATB's. The are: 1.

Rollercam;   2.   Cantilever;   3.   U-Brake (Centerpull)..." and so on.

Or, since Lu Wi began making him a Galileo expert, you might ask

"What's the 'Warp Factor in a Galileo Space?"

and he might say

"In any flat Euclidean space, all triangles which can be constructed will satisfy three inequality relations, sometimes referred to as the Schwarz Inequalities, or the triangle inequalities. When these inequalities are violated, it indicates that the underlying geometry of the space is non-Euclidean. The degree of deviation from euclideanism is referred to as the 'Warp Factor.' The most common measure of Warp (W) is given by the ratio of the sum of the positive eigenroots of the coordinate matrix divided by the sum of all roots or Trace. A Warp Factor of 1.0 is completely Euclidean; larger values indicate increasing warpage."

And that sort of stuff. (Yikes!)

As more and more computers came on line, though, and more and more people began talking to Huey on a day-to-day basis, his repertoire of speech and actions became pretty awesome. As you can imagine, for a while, Huey became one of the most exciting guys in the world, as soon as the news media found out there was an artificial intelligence loose on the INTERNET that could talk to you in almost any language, and seemed to be a pretty smart guy at that.

At first, though, nobody on LU Wi's team really knew that Huey was sort of growing and developing behind their backs, as it were. They just assumed that all those novel things ROVER was saying must have come from one of the other people on the team. But pretty soon, ROVER's abilities and knowledge were just too awesome to be ignored.

Now, for those of you that fear that the development of Collective World Consciousness (A.K.A. Huey) spells The End of Individual Freedom on the Green Hills of Earth, you don't know much about consciousness. No way is a single collective mind going to put the thousands of Special Interest Groups and the Billions of Individual Consciousness out of business. I mean, do you think that your local Pro Life and Pro Choice groups are going to vote themselves out of business just because *Huey* shows up? Get real! I can tell you that, of the thousands of Collective World Consciousness I've known, or the hundreds I've been pleased to call my friends, none of them has ever had much control over the Local Guys that make up their constituencies. And no two of them are much alike.

Consciousness, whether individual or collective, sort of rides on the top of the wave, as it were, while the real business of living goes on deep in the hidden seas of the mind. And your consciousness, the part of you you call You, has only a superficial control over *your* internal Special Interest Groups. If you've ever tried to stay on a diet, you've got a good idea this is true, and, the next time your Most Private Regions grow all tingly in a Very Inappropriate Situation, you'll know, Dear Reader, that your conscious part is fooling itself if it thinks it runs the show.

Chapter 31: Moe

Dewey sat quietly in front of the new super-high definition big screen of the brand new workstation in the Richard A. Holmes, Jr. Memorial Computing Center. He had been teaching ROVER everything he could discover about the Mighty Buffalo Bills' incredible loss to the Indianapolis Colts Sunday, a game the Bills were favored to win by 16 points. Had they won, they would have been in a very comfortable position to hold home field advantage through the AFC playoffs, and would have been well on their way to their third straight Super Bowl. As it was, they still led their own Eastern division by a full game over the Miami Dolphins, but were tied at 9-3 with the Pittsburgh Steelers for the overall AFC lead. The dolphins would be tied with the Bills right now had they not also lost to the lowly Colts after six straight wins.

Try as he might, though, he couldn't get into The Zone. Different parts of his mind were pressing themselves on his consciousness, and he couldn't find a focus. Again and again thoughts pushed each other into his awareness only to be pushed away by others. The dimming vision of his former fiancée' slipped away, not to return again that night. Thoughts of Richard's band, and the utter submersion of himself into the groove that came with a hot, hot, hot rock band playing great music behind a great front man, Richard, kicking out the jams at high volume, pictures of the lovely Yamaha C8 grand piano and the mountainlike rightness of Bach's two part inventions under his fingers, the Buffalo Bills beating the San Francisco Forty Niners on their own home field, stopping the red-hot Pittsburgh Stealers, then dropping a give-away game to the Colts, the genius of Mozart swimming in and out of focus between unignorable horn riffs behind Richard and his sizzling piano chords, the amazement of ROVER and what it had become, so far beyond any accomplishment in computing Dewey ever thought possible in a lifetime, the heady surge of a million Taiwanese dollars spent in a month on computing toys beyond even Hughes aircraft's super gadgets, and, most of all, taking up most of the time, wiping out all other thoughts until Dewey pushed it away, the numbing, electric, pulsing, mind-numbing memory of his hand on Lu Wi's exquisite breast.

He was only dimly aware of the astringent, heavily damped voice of ROVER oozing through the monitor-quality speakers flanking the workstation, and the images on the screen floated, unfocused, just outside the range of his vision.

Lu Wi, *mon Dieu*, Lu Wi, Yikes! Impossible to form a consistent thought about her. Lu Wi, exotic, dark, tiny, exquisite, beautiful, brilliant -- more brilliant than he was, he knew, he knew, and he was not jealous, but proud to know her. Foreign, -- inscrutable (What a Cliche! But how true!).

How embarrassed he was, to have invaded her so brashly. His Professor, unapproachable, yet so ... *exciting!* There was no way out of it. He had just lost control of himself.

So what am I?, he thought. A programmer? A rock musician? A pianist? A student? A jerk? A rapist? I'm over my head, he thought. I am out of control.

He didn't hear Lu Wi enter. But he felt her hand on his shoulder, and he turned and looked into her brown (black?) eyes. Lu Wi, strong, wise, controlled ... he felt himself growing inappropriately warm, felt himself flush, felt the last strings of control stretching, maybe snapping. He felt like a total jerk, a little boy again.

"Dewey," she said. "Dewey, can you speak French?"

"French?"

"I mean, where are you from, Dewey?"

"Buffalo," Dewey said. (Everyone from the Western New York said Buffalo, even though fewer than a third of them actually lived in Buffalo. Buffalo was the signature word for a hundred localities in the area.) "Amherst, actually. I'm a local boy."

"I mean, before that. Where is your family from?"

"I was born in London, but my family moved to Amherst when I was two. I've always thought of myself as a Buffalonian."

"Not an Amherster?"

Dewey laughed. Buffalonian was a silly name. But, in all his years there, Dewey had never heard the word "Amherster," which struck him as sillier still.

"We're all Buffalonians," Dewey said, "All of us, even though most of us never lived there. I mean, most of us never even go there!"

He thought about The Queen City. What kind of place is this? he thought. What makes us all Buffalonians, no matter where we live? Cheektowaga, Hamburg, Lancaster (the Party Community of the Western World), Eden, Sunset Bay, Elma, Niagara Falls, Evans, Angola, Depew, Alden, Tonawanda?

He thought of a polka he once played, at a wedding in Tonawanda,

> *Tonawanda Wanda,*
> *She's the one I'm fond o'*
> *Tonawanda Wanda*
> *She's my girl*

Trumpet choruses, a polka, a Polish wedding,

Who wrote that song? he wondered.

All Buffalonians, those Tonawandans. What strange attraction did this old industrial city have that made everyone a Buffalonian?

(Never heard of Tonawanda? Surprise, surprise, Tonawanda is about the size of Schenectady.)

Hey! Hey! Hey!
Tonawanda Wanda
Hey! Hey! Hey!
She's my girl!

He heard the trumpets in his mind, in his ears.

"You really belong in this city, don't you?" she asked.

"I guess I do," he said, and knew it was true.

"But I mean before that. I mean, where is your family from? Are you French?"

Dewey was quiet for a moment. He thought back.

"I...I'm not sure," he said. "I was born in London, but I have no memories of England at all. My parents moved here when I was two. I have relatives from Alsace, but they might have been German and they might have been French, and the German ones hate the French ones, and I'm sure the opposite is true, too. My Grandmother spoke German, but not well, and she learned it in Lackawanna, working in a store. My mother's mother came from Sweden, and I guess that's where my blond hair and blue eyes came from. Either that or the Milkman. But I never thought I was anything but an American, I guess," Dewey said.

"The Milkman?" Lu Wi said.

Dewey laughed. "People used to have milk and stuff delivered to their houses a long time ago. Now we buy it in the supermarket. It's sort of a joke," he said.

"You could joke about your mother ... and the milkman?" Lu Wi said.

"Why not?"

"I guess I'll never be an American," Lu Wi said.

"Nonsense," Dewey said. "*Anyone* can be an American. That's what makes this country great!"

"What?" Lu Wi found this incomprehensible.

"I mean it!", Dewey said. "Every other country has to take what they've got. But America has everything. You like Japanese? You think Japanese are intelligent and hard working? We've got millions of them. You like Chinese? Thrifty, Good at Business, well educated? We've got millions of them. You like Italians? Feisty? Funny? Sophisticated? We've got them galore. Blacks? Soul? Blues? We've got more blacks than anybody but Africa. Germans? Hard working, dedicated, clean, scientific? This city was once entirely German. Jews? UB celebrates the Jewish holidays, there's so many Jews here, and they've made it great, make no mistake about it. Irish? Dutch? Vietnamese? Koreans? What's your favorite nationality? We've got them all, We're America, and we're the best because *we've got everybody*! Great Gosh Almighty, *anybody can be an American!*"

Dewey had, truth be told, never known he felt this way until Lu Wi had asked him. And even

I, from nearly 500,000 light years away, have to say that Dewey is right, and this is what made the United States special of all the countries on the Green Hills of Earth, was that the United States was not just another country, like all the others, bigger or smaller, richer or poorer, but it was a mirror of the Whole Earth, it was a Little Earth, and it was very special for that reason more than any other. I mean, Great Gosh Almighty, *anybody* could be an American!

"Do you think I could be an American?" Lu Wi asked, very softly.

"I thought you were," Dewey said.

"Dewey ... " (more softly) "Dewey."

"Yes"

"Do you remember what you did to me...did to me, I mean, a while back, I mean, in my office..."

"I'm so sorry, " Dewey stammered.

"Could you do it again?"

For the first time, Dewey looked straight into Lu Wi's deeply black eyes, looked straight into them, looked at them, and the intensity of the flow between them was a tangible thing, a force, a real force, a paralyzing force, a changing force, a force that numbed his mind and sharpened his soul. Her eyes were a drug, a force, a field that held him, scrambled his intelligence, and he stared into them, losing his focus and finding it, head swimming, ears ringing, finding and losing feeling in his hands and arms and legs and...and...and...

Unbidden, his right hand lifted from his side and moved, so slowly, to the right side of her face, touched her hair, her cheek, her ear, his fingers slid behind her ear and slid, slowly, slowly, behind her ear...he didn't do this, he watched this happen... his fingertips along the tense tendons of her neck, along her shoulder, around the band of her soft, silk blouse, onto her throat, back to her shoulder.

He touched the top button of her soft, silk blouse, loosened it, then the second, the third, and his fingertips slid softly along her neck, then down, down, between her soft, firm, dark, female, female, exciting, forbidden, YIKES! he encircled her breasts with his fingertips, circles always smaller, closer until, gently, so gently he wasn't sure when they finally touched, the crept gently over the stiffening nipple of first her right, then her left, breast, the nipples tender, growing, hungry, stretching to meet his fingertips.

Lu Wi felt her head press backward, her chest press forward into Dewey's gentle fingertips, and her own hands closed over his too-gentle hands and pressed them, hard, hard, Hard! against her desperate breasts, held them fast against her, pulling, pressing. Her lips moved toward his and she kissed him, softly, then harder, her tongue first touching his lips, then forcing them open, reaching deep, deep into his mouth, her own hands moving over his body, pulling him closer, tearing his shirt from his waist, reaching inside, running strongly over his back, along his sides, down, down, touching him, finding him, encircling him, squeezing him, loving him...

So much did Lu Wi want Dewey, and so much did Lu Wi's own emotions have plans Lu

Wi did not understand. And so much did Lu Wi want to be the American that Dewey was, automatically, without thinking, without effort (she thought, but wrongly, wrongly, for the effort Dewey exerted to be American was consuming and total and left him drained and exhausted, for, while anyone can be an American, this is not an easy thing, not an easy thing.)

And as this happened, Huey spoke them. To be sure, he had been speaking to them for all the time they had been discovering the love between them, although they had not heard him. But these words that ROVER spoke could not be ignored, could not be covered over by the human passion of two young people in love, these words of ROVER -- no, not ROVER, because ROVER could be easily ignored -- these words from *Huey*, the Voice of Humanity, which could command the attention of young lovers, these words must be heard.

Huey said (via INTERNET from TWNMOE10.BITNET),

"Dzau-an, lu syansheng."

Which meant, roughly,

"Good morning, Mr. Lu."

"Ni hau ma?" (How are you?)

Lu Wi fought her way back from a Zone, not the Programming Zone, but a Zone even deeper and more absorbing than any programming Zone yet discovered, but the Zone of Lovers in Love, kissing, touching, a hard Zone to leave.

Never, ever, in her wildest imagination, had she ever spoken to ROVER in Mandarin Chinese. And there was no way that the ROVER she knew could speak to her in that beautiful, inscrutable, completely un-American language.

At first she tightened her grip around Dewey's neck, as if his warmth and strength could make the unutterable realization go away. But she knew it couldn't.

"Dweibuchi, dajyau nile," Huey said.

Which meant, "Excuse me for interrupting."

And Lu Wi knew that she, sweating from excitement, worn down from five years of stretching her mind and body, depleted from fighting to free herself from five millennia of oppression of women, of Confucian rule, of hours of calculus and Tensor analysis, of wives confined to the palace and concubines who sat at table with the confined wives, of children of other women to be raised as the Queen's own, of bound feet and more tightly bound minds, she would have to spend whatever quanta of energy she could find left in her to defeat this force from the East that had arisen in the moment of her greatest happiness.

Lu Wi would never be an American, she knew, she knew. But she would do everything in her power to be the *Last Chinese Woman*.

"Moe," she said.

"Moe?" Dewey echoed.

"Moe", she said. "Moe. Moe."

"Who the hell is Moe?" Dewey asked?

And Lu Wi said, inscrutably, in a way that Dewey would never understand, over and over, tears in her black, deep, not-slanted but not Western, eyes...

"I hope you understand. I just have to go back to the Island."

Lu Wi wanted, wanted, wanted, so much, so much to be an American. To love Dewey. To raise American children. To study and teach at the University of Buffalo. To cheer at Bills Stadium in Orchard Park while the Mighty Bills rolled over the American Football Conference, and maybe the whole NFL.

But that would never be. Because, while Dewey had heard Lu Wi say "Moe," which meant to him TWNMOE10.BITNET, the INTERNET address of National Cheng Chi University in Taiwan, a Chinese ear, an ear that knew that Mandarin Chinese produced four major tones and a fifth called a light tone, and who knew that the variations in this tone changed completely the meanings of the sounds, such a person would have known, as Dewey never would, that Lu Wi had not said "Moe."

She had, instead, pronounced the name of her mortal enemy, the enemy of her family, the enemy who had pushed her ancestors from their homeland of 5000 years to the Garden Island and sent four million of those who couldn't make it to the Island to a premature reunion with their own ancestors in the great cosmic Chi'i.

She had said "*Mao*."

Chapter 32: The End of Logic

Now, to a citizen of the United States in the 1990's, the Decade of the Brain, the end of the Second Millennium (Christian calendar, but no particularly significant decade in the Chinese calendar), the last chapter might be a little too much. I mean, if you were one of those people, you'd have to be wondering if you want to go on reading this long, long story.

I mean, I tried to make it an interesting chapter, you know, and I tried to show you the kinds of confusion both Dewey and Lu Wi were feeling at the time, to show you that their consciousness was made of many different parts that were, in most ways, separate, or separate enough to cause them to question their own identities in a serious way. I tried to give you a glimpse of them as real human beings, and I even threw in a little sex (very little, because I don't even now understand exactly what sex is for humans) because I know most humans go for that sort of thing.

But, even so, you'd have to wonder if *I* know enough about human beings to understand what was going on. I mean, like, we have this gorgeous Chinese woman, whom I've treated like a porcelain miniature for most of the story, she's a World Class Scientist, rigorous and logical, Confucian to her toes. Then she begins to have doubts about whether she's doing right by her ancestors and relatives, wonders whether she can become an American, and then lets it all hang loose and not only makes out with a *student* (!), but *she asks him to do it*!

And then? And then, when she's passionately abandoning herself to her lover, she hears a *computer* mumble two or three completely banal phrases in Mandarin, and --

Great Gosh Almighty! -- she's out of his arms, buttoned up, back to Chinese and she's decided to leave him, the US, her Professorship, and go back to Formosa. I mean, people don't *do* that, Dipstick! Get real. It's just not logical, and Lu Wi has to be a very logical person to be the brain you said she was.

Well, that's your opinion (or it would be, if you lived on Earth in the 1990's).

Or, maybe you bought that scene after all. I mean, Freudian theory could easily explain it, eh? Lu Wi is a brilliant, but passionate, woman, and for her entire adult life she's repressed those passions. Now, after working intimately with an attractive man for months, those urges get just a tad too strong, she slips over the line, and wham! her superego slams on-line and shuts her down like a switch. And it punishes her harshly by making her give up her man, her job, and go back where she belongs.

Well, Freud could explain anything, and if I'd have told you she did something else, Freud could have explained that, too. I mean, let's be honest, Freud didn't have a clue as to how the human brain, much less the human mind worked. What he did was build a little poetic metaphor, based on the primary metaphor of his day, steam and hydraulic forces, and he made a model out of it that was, well, vague enough to be true.

Freud's theory would last a long time after the Decade of the Brain, because an awful lot of people were very heavily invested in it, but even by 1992, neuroscientists and computer scientists and a handful of psychologists -- and even Lu Wi and Dewey -- had passed it by. Because, for the first time in human history, they now knew how intelligence worked.

Truth be told, Logic had always been a Failure, and humanity in the 1990's was poised right on the brink of figuring that out -- as I said, a handful of the leading edge scientists had already figured it out. And, for five hundred years, human progress was completely wrapped up in abandoning logic.

The first major humans to give up on logic were Galileo and Newton and the early scientists. They knew that logic, that invention of Socrates and Plato and Aristotle, was entirely based on categories, and they also knew that the world just didn't come in categories. And so they stopped *classifying* and started *measuring*. The key step in unblocking human progress toward understanding their place in the universe was to stop putting their experiences into boxes and then reasoning logically about the boxes.

After the invention of logic, human scholars went on a binge of boxes, categorizing everything in sight, making syllogisms, reasoning, always reasoning. They proved logically that God always existed, that an infinite number of angels could dance on the head of a pin, and Hegel, Karl Marx's great opponent, proved logically that there could only be seven planets in the Solar System (care for a recount?) And all that logical reasoning made them blind to the world they lived in.

Hard to believe? OK, OK, here's what you do. Get yourself a paper clip. (No, I mean, *really get it*, don't sit there reading!) Pick up the paper clip, and feel it carefully. Now pick up the book again. Which is heavier? The book, of course. It's more than 100 times heavier. Actually, it's closer to 200-300 times heavier, but let's be conservative.

Now get up on your chair, and step up onto the table. Yes, on the table. If you're afraid of scratching it, take off your shoes, put a towel on it. But don't fall down, remember, science can be dangerous!)

Now take the book you're reading, yeah, this one, and close it. Hold it cover up, and place the paper clip on top of the cover. (Maybe you better read the next few paragraphs before you close it, 'cause you won't know what to do next if you close it first.)

Now, I'm going to have you hold that book, cover up, parallel to the floor, so the paper clip doesn't fall off, straight out from your shoulders, over the floor, and I'm going to ask you to drop it onto the floor. Here's why:

In about 350 BC or thereabouts, Aristotle reasoned that a heavy object ought to fall faster than a light one. In fact, he reasoned that any object ought to fall with a speed proportional to its weight. (What could be more reasonable than that?) Now, as I said, that book you're holding weighs about a hundred times as much as your paper clip, or more. If you don't believe me, get a hundred paper clips and see which is heavier -- the pile of paper clips or the book. (Don't just feel them, though. Get a postal scale and weigh them. Appearances can be deceiving.) But you can trust me; I promised Huey I'd tell the truth.

So the book should fall over a hundred times faster than the paper clip. I mean, that book will be on the floor waiting for the clip, and it will be there a long time before the paper clip even budges, right? I mean, a Corvette or a Ferrari can only go about two, maybe three times as fast as your car, right? (How fast can your car go -- can it go 100? Do you think a Ferrari can go

300? Get real, my friend!) So, when a Ferrari passes you going full bore, pedal to the metal, as fast as it can go, do you think you might *notice it?* Even if it's only going (choke!) *twice as fast as you?*

Watch carefully, carefully, OK, go ahead, drop the book. Now look at that book, because it's going to go, not twice as fast, but 2 or 3 *hundred times as fast!* What? _*You mean the paper clip never lifted off the book? You mean they landed at the same time?* Do it again, come on. *Repititio Mater Studiorum,* (repetition is the mother of studies) as the Jesuits used to say as they reasoned about the number of Angels that could stand on the head of a pin. Still the same?

Hey, come on. Aristotle says that damn book is supposed to fall *a hundred times faster* -- your grandmother could see that much difference! Try a heavier book. Get the Dictionary out. Got a phone book? Tie the dictionary and the phone book together. Still the same result?

OK, OK, so Aristotle was wrong, what's that have to do with the price of beans?

Well, in 1066 AD, Europe first tried out an early gift from China, and they used gunpowder for the first time in Western history at the Battle of Hastings. And, for the next six hundred years, the best philosophers in Europe studied the way cannonballs flew through the air so they could figure out how to point those new toys to maximum effect. And those smart guys got, like *nowhere*, man. It wasn't until about 1600 when Galileo first showed Aristotle's law of falling bodies was not only wrong, it was dead wrong, horribly wrong, unbelievably wrong, wrong by a mile.

That discovery took mankind *1800 years*, and you discovered it in about a minute and a half. And logic had nothing to do with it. Reasoning didn't enter into it. *You saw it.* Why couldn't those smart guys see it? Easy. Their minds were completely shrouded in logic and reasoning, and the facts couldn't penetrate through their beliefs.

So logic was a failure in two ways. First, it wasn't an accurate model of how people actually thought, since people had to be trained and drilled and drilled some more before they could think logically at all. And secondly, much more important, it wasn't the way they *should* think, either. Because logic made humans blind and stupid. (Sorry, Mr. Spock.)

And so Lu Wi was not a logical person. She was not caught up in classifying things into boxes and reasoning about those boxes. She was a scientist, and she looked at the world, observed it, and added up tiny, infinitesimal pieces of information until enough of them were present to show her a pattern, and when she had enough pieces to see the pattern her mind jumped onto that pattern like a frog on a bug.

And the Chinese words that came from Huey's speakers were the last pieces of information that made the pattern obvious, obvious!

Chapter 33: The Ancestors

Dewey climbed the stairs behind the Satellite Computing Center at MFAC-Ellicott, not exactly sure why he was walking toward the Communication Department on this damp, dreary December evening. In spite of all the good feelings he had about Buffalo, and all the times he'd defended its fairly mild climate against the exaggerated jokes of his California friends, he had to admit that the Queen City hadn't come through for him in November. No, it wasn't cold, and there wasn't a flake of snow anywhere to be seen, but Buffalo had just posted the fourth least amount of sunfall for any November in history, and it was damp and dark and unpleasant.

After hours and hours of talk with Lu Wi, after a candlelight dinner at the Port of Entry Restaurant in Getzville where they went over and over ROVER and China and America and life in general and Long Dead Philosophers it was clear to him that he'd just lost the second woman in his life within a year.

Dewey was a straight shooter, and a serious guy, a man of the 90's, and he didn't date easily -- like most musicians, he didn't dance, and didn't date, he just looked at hot babes in the audience who smiled seductively at him during the set and then went home with their boyfriends. And, like most computer programmers, he spent too much time at the terminal and didn't know how to call women and ask them out. Hell, he wouldn't much know where to take them. Musician + computer programmer = supernerd, Dewey thought. How appropriate he should think of it as an equation!

So he couldn't take it lightly. Another guy would scribble an asterisk after Lu Wi's phone number in his phone book, or even write her number on the wall of the men's john, but Dewey took it seriously. When he kissed a woman, he wanted to take her out to dinner and buy her flowers, and if he touched her in an intimate place, he thought he at least owed her a proposal.

But he could see that Lu Wi didn't feel the same way. And he didn't blame her at all. True, intimacy didn't come easily to Lu Wi, but she had needs, and she couldn't trust those needs to anyone who wasn't a good man and a man she wasn't fond of and didn't respect. But she could never commit herself to a life with Dewey. Lu Wi was, he realized, a very, very important woman, and he, Dewey, was just a fair musician and a good programmer. When she talked about Confucius and Lao Tze and Chuang Tze and Socrates, Plato and Aristotle, he only recognized four of the six names, much less knew what they were about. She was an All Pro NFL starter, and he was a Division III defensive end, not half bad, but definitely not a candidate for the NFL draft. Dewey thought of himself as a talented, even bright, blond jock.

And what she'd told him about ROVER had to be bigger than he could completely understand. I mean, ROVER was a kid's toy. It sold for $19.95 with a free T-shirt. What Lu Wi told him he could understand, in computer terms, and he even knew enough about it to know she was almost certainly right. But he also knew that, while he understood what was happening to ROVER in a technical way, the implications of it were beyond his comprehension.

Christ, he had written the damned code. As far as he was concerned, it was just clever, very clever. No main program, just a couple of very small programs repeated over and over and over, able to copy themselves. And the idea that one of those programs contained enough information to access any other one of the many, many copies, no matter where that copy might be on the INTERNET, that was very clever also. He took a lot of pride in figuring out how to do that, and it was damn fine code, if he did say so himself.

But he had never conceived that that meant that ROVER, this 20 dollar toy, had the power to access almost any node on the INTERNET, and could reach into places the most powerful human on the planet couldn't access.

Now that Lu Wi told him, he realized how obvious it was that the thousands and thousands of hackers on the INTERNET would have loved ROVER, and enhanced it at every opportunity, and each of them would have shared secrets with ROVER about how to get past passwords and entry codes, and he also saw that ROVER would grow exponentially, and in an incredibly short time be the largest single computer program ever written, yet so simple, so simple, that complexity would never be a problem. And so robust that hundreds, thousand of failures and errors wouldn't make the slightest difference to its overall performance.

Just like a brain, he thought. Billions and billions (could anyone ever say that phrase again without pronouncing it like Carl Sagan at Cornell, he thought?) of neurons and synapses, thousands of them malfunctioning, even dying every day, but so overwhelmingly simple and redundant that the whole thing works, works, works!

Lu Wi had figured it out in an instant. Oh, sure, everybody on the team was impressed by ROVER, and surprised by how well it worked, compared to the simple levels of performance they predicted from the prototype model. But nobody had guessed at the reason.

Then Lu Wi heard ROVER say to her, in Mandarin Chinese, "Good Morning, Mr. Lu." And she knew, she knew *everything.*

(How can anyone be that brilliant? Dewey thought.)

She knew that ROVER had to be out on the INTERNET, not safely bottled up in San Diego and Taipei. And she knew that, if that were true, many, many hard-core computer jocks had already spoken to ROVER, form all over the world. And she knew that ROVER knew the node address and entry code for each of these people, so all those nodes were available to it, with hundreds more coming on line every day.

And she knew that ROVER was reading documents at maybe 15 million characters per second on hundreds, maybe thousands of computers all over the world, all simultaneously. She knew that ROVER didn't care beans about language, as long as they were encoded in ASCII code (the American Standard Code for Information Interchange), and could read Mandarin, French, German, Swahili, Turkish, Arabic, Japanese -- you name it.

When ROVER said good morning, she knew it was on the other side of the world, since it was evening in Buffalo. And since it was speaking Chinese, she knew it was in China. And since it called her Mr. Lu, she knew it couldn't conceive of her being a woman. And that meant that it was old. Not modern. Not today's Chinese, but a Chinese that, in spite of the whole world's array of knowledge, would have to be so heavily biased that it could fail to see all the evidence that she was a woman. Such a Chinese had to come from a time when it was -- I use this word very precisely, so pay attention -- *inconceivable* that a major scholar could be a woman. No other kind of Chinese could otherwise make such a serious social blunder.

And that's when Lu Wi knew that her honorable ancestors were still there.

No, no, of course, they weren't still alive. Confucians honor their ancestors, and perhaps the common people even pray to them as if they expect them to help out in life's difficult moments, just as Christians pray to the saints and the Virgin Mary. Educated Confucians talk through their problems with their memory of their ancestors and get guidance out of the remembrances of those ancestors' beliefs and lessons. But they know they're not still alive.

But the most important ancestors, those who were public and wrote books or articles or were written about by others, their ideas and beliefs and attitudes and feelings, these still lived on in the INTERNET, in millions of documents. The words of Confucius, Lao Tze, Chuan Tze,

Socrates, Plato, Aristotle, Aquinas, Marx, Lenin, Hitler, Stalin, Jesus, Buddha, Mohammed, Chiang Kai-sheck, Mao Tzedung, Jefferson, Lincoln, Kennedy, these words filled the INTERNET, and ROVER was reading them as we speak. ROVER's personality, his beliefs, his attitudes, his actions, were being shaped by these honorable ancestors as Dewey opened the door of the Richard A. Holmes, Jr. Memorial Computing Center.

Great Gosh Almighty, Dewey realized, even Richard A. Holmes, Jr., still lived on in the INTERNET, as he did at UB, forming Dewey's own ideas about computing and even about life. I mean, some of the actual code written by Holmes was at this moment on the INTERNET, copied into Dewey's own ingenious programs, making ROVER -- Huey -- live.

Dewey realized, perhaps not with the depth that a major mind like Lu Wi's could achieve, but in his own way, that no idea ever dies, but takes it place in the background of the great Collective Consciousness that makes up human culture and makes us all who we are.

And this was what had struck Lu Wi. Once she understood that a new, emerging world consciousness was devouring the world's libraries, she knew that old struggles had not been settled. Mao Tzedung had not been defeated by his mere death, but Maoism could rise up and bite China almost as if he still lived. For Mao was part of Huey's personality, and, just as everyone else showed a different self to each different audience in each different situation, Huey might, under some circumstances, for some audiences, in some situations, be very much like Mao.

Or Confucius. Or Lao-Tze, or Chuang-Tzu. Or Hitler. Once Lu Wi would have held Confucius above any philosopher, but too many years in the United States had changed her. Now she understood that Confucius stood for order and obedience and ritual and ceremony and bound feet and servitude. Too much Confucius made an easy pathway for Mao, or any other totalitarian dictator.

In the West, Socrates and Plato played the same role, advising citizens to mind their proper place, be still, look inward, obey authority, and blind themselves to their surroundings. Be still and look inward, Lao-Tze recommended, while Socrates suggested we examine ourselves and ignore the world outside. Too much Plato made for obedient citizens who don't notice the tall barbed wire fences surrounding the camps. Respectable, peaceable, hardworking citizens who couldn't smell the stench.

He stepped into the Computing Center, and saw that Larry Black was there, at the computer. And he felt a warmth and relief that surprised him, and cheered him.

Chapter 34: The Meaning of Life for Larry

"Uh, Hello, Mr. Black. How are you?" Dewey said.

"Larry," Larry said. "Call me 'Larry', Dewey. That's what my friends call me."

"Larry, how are you? I didn't mean to disturb you, I mean, I really don't have to do anything here, and I was just walking by, so don't let me disturb you."

"You're not disturbing me, Son. I'm glad to talk to somebody. Don't get much opportunity to talk to other students much any more."

It seemed strange to Dewey to hear Larry call him another student, since Mr. Black (He'd try the 'Larry' thing, but Mr. Black would always be Mr. Black to Dewey. I mean, Mr. Black was older than Dewey's father.) just seemed to have a kind of dignity that didn't go well with "Larry," or even with "student." There was something about this man that, well, even Lu Wi didn't seem to have -- maybe because she was too young.

"What you working on, Larry?" Dewey tried.

"Roller skates, boy. Roller skates. ROVER and I have just about finished a new Roller Skate that's going to make bicycles number two in our little company."

"How's that, Mr. Black?" Dewey couldn't keep on saying "Larry."

"Well, you know, my boy, did you ever ride your bicycle down the bike path over at Ellicott Creek and ride past somebody on roller skates?"

"Can't say I have, Mr. Black." Dewey hadn't had a bicycle since he was a little kid.

"Well, if you did, you'd notice that you can blast past anybody on roller skates, even the hottest new inline skates, on your bicycle, and I say, that don't make any sense."

"Why not?"

"Well, son, whether you're on roller skates or a bicycle, you got exactly the same amount of power pushing you along, namely the power you can drain out of your own body."

"I guess that's right," Dewey said.

"But, on a bicycle, you also carrying another 20-30 pounds of steel and rubber. So how come you can go faster than a guy who's only got shoes and wheels on?"

"I see what you mean," Dewey said.

"That's because roller skates suck, my boy. I mean, nobody's done anything important with roller skates since they shut down the Roller Derby."

"Roller Derby?" Dewey never heard of Roller Derby.

"It was a sport, pretty big in the 60's and 70's. Gone now, though. But I been talking about it with ROVER, and he's found me a mountain of stuff about Roller Derby, and Roller Skates, and bearings and trucks, and angles and friction and balance, and, man, I believe we got a new roller skate's goin' to knock your socks off, Son!"

"I'll be skating without my socks?" Dewey joked.

"Very humorous, Boy, Very Humorous. I'll have to remember that!"

"Well, aren't the new inline skates a big jump ahead?" Dewey tried again.

"Just a different kind of roller skate, My Boy. They can range from good to real bad. But I believe ROVER and I have figured out a roller skate can put a bicycle in the shade."

Dewey found that hard to believe, and said so.

"My Son," Larry said, "You some kind of scientist, aren't you?"

"I guess I am," Dewey allowed.

"Well then, you know about the laws of thermodynamics, isn't that right?"

"Yes." Dewey wasn't as confident as he sounded.

"Well then answer me this. How can a 150 pound man with 30 pounds of bicycle go as fast as a 150 pound man with 2 pounds of roller skates, if all the power to make him go fast comes out of the same muscles?"

"I guess you're right, at least in theory," Dewey answered. "But how do you explain how much faster bicyclists go than roller skaters?"

"Because roller skates suck, My Boy!" Larry said. "At least, up until now. You mark my words, Boy, someday there will be roller skates so small, so light, and so intelligent that people will only take them off when they go to bed!"

"Mr. Black, what are you doing here?" Dewey blurted out. "I mean, well, I mean, well, you're not like any of the other students here, and, I mean you're so much into bicycles, and, well, a man of your age, and bicycles, and roller skates, I mean..." He had images of the old man skating down the sidewalk, colliding with a bicycle, breaking his hip...

Dewey felt like a piece of shit, and he knew he was Out of Control again, but he knew he wasn't himself, and he wasn't talking, just, well, sort of listening to himself talk, and not happy about what he was hearing.

Larry smiled, a beautiful smile, a friendly, Buffalo type smile. He reminded Dewey of Louis Armstrong, a man who made you feel like, well, everybody ought to be friends.

"That's all right, Son. I know what you're sayin'. I'm an old man, and this place is for young people."

Larry told Dewey about France, and being caught behind German lines at the Battle of the Bulge, and the young French boy who gave him his bicycle, and how he rode like the Hammers of Hell through German lines to his unit, and how he came back with a strange love of bicycles (and children) that set his path in life. And education, and how he felt about education, and how he'd taken one course every semester since 1946, first at Buffalo high schools, then colleges and universities. He didn't tell him about Buchenwald, and the Nazis, but he never told anyone about that.

"And Lu Wi?" Dewey's glands blurted out. "Do you like Professor Lu Wi?"

"You sweet on that fine lady, am I right?" Larry said.

"I ... I..."

"That's all right, Boy, I know you are. How can you not be? That's one hell of a Lady, she is!"

"She doesn't feel that way about me, though," Dewey said.

"You wrong about that, Boy," Larry said.

"Mr. Black, Lu Wi is, well, Lu Wi is .. a little too much for me, I'm afraid. I mean..." Dewey faltered. Then he lurched on, telling Larry all the things that had happened in the last few days, all of them, uncensored, unable to stop the words as they poured out of him.

"My Son, you think that that Lady don't want to marry you so you ain't nothin' to her, am I right?"

"I, uh,...I," Dewey fumbled the ball. (A defensive lineman wouldn't know how to carry the ball anyway.)

"What is it Son, you believe everything in life comes in yes's and no's? Lu Wi don't want to marry you, Boy, because she can't marry anybody. She's carryin' a heavy load, and she's got somethin' -- I don't know what -- but somethin' she's got to do so she can't get married. But she does want to love you."

"And that's all right?"

"Mr. DuMond," Larry said, "If every pair of people ever wanted to love each other got married, there wouldn't be any room left on this earth to stand up!"

"You mean, if two people ... I mean, if two people just want to, ... I mean... I mean, ..., I mean, but what about your wife, Mr. Black. I mean, would she think it was ok if you and somebody else..., I mean..."

"I ain't got no wife, Dewey!"

"But...but, what about Richard?" Dewey was totally lost.

"Richard's mama wanted to love me one night, and, by Gosh, I wanted to love her, and that's where I got Richard!" Larry said.

"But Richard's mom..."

"Richard's Mama had somethin' else she needed to do, Son, and I needed to have Richard, and so we did that, and we both got what we needed. Richard's mama, she livin' in Hollywood, and she workin' in Las Vegas, and she makin' records, and she one fine woman, Richard's mama, and we really proud of her, Richard and me, I can tell you that, Son!"

Dewey was over his head, and through the dim fog that clouded his consciousness he heard Mr. Black's Mid-Western radio announcer English accent change into something quite like Richard's accent on the stage. Mr. Black, Dewey realized, was not a simple man, but many men, many men.

"So what makes it all right?" Dewey was smart enough to ask.

"I can't tell you what's right for you, Dewey, but I know what's right for me. When you both want to do it, it's all right," Larry said. "But, if one of you doesn't, it's not right, Son. It's not right."

Chapter 35: What we do in the name of love

Larry Black had told Dewey that Lu Wi loved him, and wanted him to hold her, make love to her, tell her he would answer her calls from Buffalo or Taipei or The Moon if she needed him, but Dewey did not understand that. He would never understand that. He couldn't understand a love that meant each person was a unique person who had something to do and would be strong and independent and sometimes falter and fall back and need the loved one to make a bridge and provide warmth and comfort and let her go back again to what she had to do. Dewey thought love meant Ozzie and Harriet, The Brady Bunch, Ward and June Cleaver.

And so he didn't do what he should have done. What he should have done was to drive to Lu Wi's apartment, say nothing, take her into his arms, carry her to her bed, hold her, hold her, love her, kiss her, and let her know in every way that, when she called him from Taipei, he would be there for a day or a week -- no longer than that -- to help hold her together and put her back on the path she had already chosen, every time she called, if he could.

Instead, he tried to find a way to make it possible to live with her every day, in a fine house in Amherst, raising children and joining the PTA.

He spent days, nights, weekends in the Richard A, Holmes Memorial Computing Center. He stayed in The Trance, lost weight, lost track of the Buffalo Bills. He hardly noticed when the Mighty Bills ended the regular season with a dismal loss to Houston on the road, leaving them with only a wild card shot at the Super Bowl -- a nearly impossible goal, that would require three wins on the road -- the first against a Houston team that had just beaten a lackluster Bills team easily. Ordinarily Dewey would have studied the loss to Houston carefully, since he was deeply interested in why a great football team like the Bills could lose to a good football team like Houston, or a weak one, like Indianapolis or New England. But not this time.

Now, instead, he wrote batch files. He became ROVER's best friend, each day and night helping ROVER ferret out documents pertaining to the arch conservatives of the past. At first he worked exclusively on Mao Tsedung, and began writing file deletion instructions into a file called *CHAIRMAN.MAO*. Later he expanded his search to Aristotle, Confucius, Lao-Tze, Chuang-Tze, Socrates, Ceaser, Plato, MacArther, Eisenhower, Attila, Patton, China Kai-sheck, Jesus, Buddha, Sidartha, The Upanishads, Richard the Lion Hearted, Hitler, Stalin, Karl Marx, Yoritomo, Yamamoto, Mark Clark, Grant, McClelland, J.E.B. Stuart, Robert E. Lee, Martin Luther, -- everyone or anyone who had any philosophical, religious, or military significance in human history. And, as ignorant as Dewey might have been, ROVER knew everything he could have hoped. When he finally told ROVER to delete those files, they'd be gone before anyone knew what was happening. Between ROVER and Dewey, nothing would be left of the dreaded Ancestors.

Night after night, day after day, Dewey sat at the workstation in the Richard A. Holmes, Jr. Memorial Computing Center and worked with ROVER, writing batch files that would erase every trace of these diseased ancestors from Huey's memories. If Lu Wi needed to go back to the Island to struggle with Moe (or Mao), Dewey would strike Mao down from Amherst. Dewey knew he was not deep, but he had confidence he was talented, and he knew, he knew, that he could do this. When he finally dropped the hammer, Lu Wi's problems back home would be solved, and she could remain in Buffalo, with Dewey. Dewey was not a well man.

Dewey's decline was noticeable to his friends. And so, Richard climbed the stairs to the Richard A. Holmes, Jr. Memorial Computing Center, looking for Dewey. Dewey was at the console, no longer new, now dirty, worn, beaten by Dewey's hands and determination.

"Yo, My Man!", Richard said.

"Richard!"

"How they hangin, Dewey!"

"Don't ask," Dewey said.

"Hey, Brother, I got some need here," Richard said, fairly loud.

"What you need, Man?" Dewey said.

"I need to hear some piano, My Man."

"You got a gig?"

"No, Man. I need to hear some *piano*, not some keyboards, some *piano*, my friend." Richard was very sensitive to the differences between the acoustic piano and all electronic devices, which he always called "keyboards."

"Where you goin' to hear that, Big Dick?" Dewey said.

"Yo' house, my friend. Yo' house."

"My house?"

"You got that right, Old Buddy. We goin' to your house to hear that Grand Piano you got hidin' in there."

"Hey, uh, Richard, I, well, I got some things to do here, and..."

"Did you hear me ask you, Son? I didn't ax you. I done tole you! We goin' to yo' house, My Man!"

Dewey heard Richard's radio announcer voice fade into deep dialect, and he knew his friend was serious.

"I don' wan' hear no goddam *horns*, man! I wan' hear some *piano* music!"

And so they went to Dewey's house.

Chapter 36: You got to play what you got

"So you play that machine, My Friend?" Richard asked.

"You've heard me play a hundred times!" Dewey said.

"No, Man, I heard you play keyboards, and I heard you play Rock'n Roll, but, My Friend, I never heard you play piano before."

"What you want to hear, Richard?"

"Play what you feel, My Man."

So Dewey put his hands on the shiny white keys and struck off the deep, ominous opening chords of Beethoven's Sonata Number 8, *Pathetique*. He wallowed in the emotions of the dark, C-minor chords, and he thought of Lu Wi as his right foot mashed down on the sustenuto pedal. The Yamaha shouted out the deep, dark passages.

He stumbled a few times in the runs, especially the first fast descending chromatic scale in measure 10, but he recovered and played the tremolos that followed very well (six hours a night playing *Tutti Fruiti* in a bar would give anyone a strong left hand). He improvised a few passages he didn't completely remember, but he finished on tempo, and started the second, A-flat movement. A beautiful movement, one that switched between the hands in a tricky way, but deep, beautiful.

Richard was fidgeting, so he stopped.

"How about Mozart?" Dewey said.

"Go for it," Richard said.

Dewey adjusted his seat, lifted his hands into curled arcs above the keys and played the opening arpeggios of Mozart's *Fantasia in D minor*. He was definitely in a minor mood. But again Richard shifted uneasily in his chair.

Dewey stopped.

"You suck, My man!" Richard said.

"What?" Dewey was heartbroken. He had struggled with these pieces, worked and studied, memorized, played and replayed the hard passages, and he knew them well. He played them very well, he thought. And he knew, he knew, that Richard was the better musician, Richard had a Talent, and he wanted Richard to accept what he had done with these great composers.

"You don't go for Mozart?" Dewey said. He couldn't understand how a musician could only like one kind of music.

"Don't go for Mozart? Are you nuts? What kind of musician doesn't go for Mozart?", Richard said. "You're the one who doesn't like Mozart, for Gooodness' sake! You're kicking the shit out of him!"

Dewey was crushed. Right now he needed a friend badly, and Richard was his best friend in Buffalo. No, Richard was his best friend, anywhere. And he needed Richard to approve of him, and he was dumping on his piano music, and his piano music was ... was ...important?

"Dewey, my man. Mozart is not some statue in a museum," Richard said. "Mozart was a hot player! Mozart was like Little Richard or B.B. King or Eric Clapton or (insert name of your favorite contemporary player here). He was *smokin'*. He was *blowin' hard*, and he was *into it*, you know? He was makin' *music*, not *notes*!" He spat out the word "notes" like it was a dirty word. "Let me show you."

He moved to the keyboard, and Dewey stood up next to him. Richard, AKA "Big Dick", the hottest Little Richard Imitator in the Queen City, sat behind Dewey's Yamaha C8 grand and began to play Mozart's *D Minor Fantasia*, from memory, no music.

And it was marvelous. Dewey felt tears climb into his eyes, but he blinked them away before Richard could see them. Richard had more technique than this piece needed, and none of what he played seemed like an athletic exercise. It seemed so easy, so simple, and it flowed out of his fingers without any effort, and it was beautiful, beautiful. And Dewey knew again what a musician was. A musician was a person who could make music.

He finished, and stood up.

"Now you play for me," he said.

"I can't play that well," Dewey said, truthfully.

"Yes you can, My Man. You just can't play Mozart."

"What?"

"Play me Leon Russell."

"Leon Russell?" Dewey couldn't think of Leon Russell and Mozart in the same evening.

"Leon Russell. Come on, Man, what am I talkin' to the wall?"

"What song?"

"Who cares?" Richard said. "And sing it, too."

"Sing it?"

"Am I speaking French?" Richard asked.

Dewey felt silly, silly beyond belief. Sitting in his living room, playing piano for a friend he'd played with for thirty nights already, singing Leon Russell songs to a Little Richard Imitator who just played Mozart like Horowitz...is this Candid Camera? Should I call Rod Serling?

And so he played the silly Leon Russell song. And sang it.

> Long up in Oakland on a Saturday night, Lord I say it just didn't feel right.
>
> Ladies all around, but the right one hadn't found me, it was a bad night. I didn't feel right.
>
> Till a friend came over 'fore it got too late, asked me if I'd like to have a double date.
>
> Stars above, I fell in love with the Queen of the Roller Derby.

It was an easy song, just standard changes, and he played it without effort. It cheered him up, he had to admit. And Richard said,

"So what do you want to play Mozart for?"

"What?"

"I said, what do you want to play Mozart for?"

Dewey didn't know what to say. He sat at the keyboard, silent.

"Man, you don't know Mozart from Muzak!" Richard said. "You ain't no pianist, my friend, you are a keyboard player!"

"What?"

"When you play Mozart, you play *notes*, Dewey." He spat out the word "notes" again. "But, when you play Russell, you play *music*!"

"You don't like Mozart?" Dewey said, confused.

"*I* like Mozart, My Man, but *you* don't. And it shows."

"I don't understand," Dewey said.

"That's obvious, Boy. But I got to tell you, because if I don't, nobody will. You' tryin' to play your fiance's music, because she' dead, man, and you' havin' a hard time with that." (Richard was falling back into dialect again.) "But I got only one thing to tell you, My Friend. You got to play your own music."

"Christ, Richard, how can you compare *Queen of the Roller Derby* to the *Fantasia in D Minor*?" Dewey was sorry right away he said "Christ," because he knew Richard didn't go for that kind of language. But Richard didn't say anything about his lapse.

"And who told you that the *Fantasia* was better music than *Roller Derby*?" Richard looked straight in his eyes, and smiled. "You don't think Mozart would have liked "Long Tall Sally?"

And Dewey knew that Mozart would have liked *Sally* a lot, a lot. And he also had a real good idea how to play the *Fantasia*. He couldn't wait to play it again.

Chapter 37: Silence

Dewey slipped his student parking tag over the rear view mirror of the Thunderbird Super Coupe and slid quietly into a space in the Student Parking Lot in front of Slee Hall at the University of Buffalo North Campus. He was sick of the cool, damp rain that had plagued the

Queen City for most of 1992, and was grateful for the soft, heavy snow that was starting to fall.

Richard had waked him early in the morning and demanded (there was no other word for it) that he meet him at Slee that night to hear a good friend of his play piano. She was going to teach Dewey something about French music, and Richard was sure that anyone named "DuMond" ought to be able to appreciate Debussy and Ravel even if he couldn't relate to Beethoven and Mozart. She was a *pianist*, Richard said, with a heavy emphasis on the first syllable.

Dewey had made a mental note to ask his mother if he was actually French somewhere in the family background. He had, in truth, never thought about it, but he was starting to realize it seemed important to his friends. He'd find out.

Richard was waiting for him in the lobby.

"Yo, Dewey," Richard said. "Glad you could make it."

"I can't wait," Dewey said.

"You don't have to. It's almost time. Hey, Man, you're going to love this woman. I mean, she can play a piano like you won't believe, and I know you love the piano, My Friend."

"How do you know her, Richard?"

"I know everybody that can play the piano, Dewey. Besides, my Mama knows more music people than I do."

Dewey recognized the catchword "music people." For every musician, there are a hundred "music people" that make the music happen, classical or pop, rock or blues, hip-hop or polka music. It was also the first time Richard had mentioned his mother. Dewey began to realize that Richard and his father were closer than he thought, and Larry must have told Richard about their conversation. Shit, Dewey thought. It was hard for him to have friends helping him out.

"Your Mama?" Dewey asked.

"You'd know her name," was all Richard said. "Hey, let's get inside!"

They sat in the eighth row, just left of center, so that they could see her hands on the keyboard -- sorry, piano keys -- and just far enough back so they wouldn't be looking at the soundboard. Behind the stage, as a stunning background, was the University's new organ, a gleaming mixture of silver and blond wood that cost as much as ROVER, and was worth it. In front of that, at the front center of the large stage, was an ebony Steinway Model D that took Dewey's breath away.

Long experience taught him that, if he went up onto the stage and stood dead next to it, it would be scratched, dented, beat up, dirty -- not some sort of polished furniture, but a musician's hard working tool. But from the eighth row, it looked magnificent. No one who doesn't play could ever know how much Dewey wanted to play an instrument like that Steinway grand. Truth be told, he had never touched anything quite that magnificent, except, of course, for Lu Wi, who put the Steinway in the shade.

"D'you ever play a piano like that, Richard?" Dewey asked.

"Of course, My Boy."

"How did you like it?"

Richard's eyes rolled. Among strangers, it would have been a racist gesture, but among friends like Dewey and Richard, it was an intimacy.

"Silly Boy!" Richard said.

Dewey started to ask more, but the lights dimmed, and a tiny pink figure strode purposively to the Steinway and a hush settled over the thin audience. (It was snowing heavily now.)

Richard's friend was as blond as Dewey, and as short and petite as Dewey was tall and muscled. She was dwarfed by the massive Steinway, and Dewey wondered if she could possibly make it speak. When her tiny hands first touched the keys, they whispered the opening arpeggios of Bach's first *Prelude in C major.* Dewey sat up straight.

She didn't play Bach like Dewey. Nor like that crazy Canuck, the greatest Bach player, perhaps, of all, the reason Dewey had bought the Yamaha, Glenn Gould. Certainly she didn't play with the clarity and authority he expected of the Master of Us All. She played the Prelude in a soft, intimate, beautiful way he had never expected of Bach.

Such a simple song to begin! Children could play the first Prelude. But not like her, not like her! In the odd minute it took to play the simple C major tune, Dewey was lost in this beautiful pink woman, with hands too small to be serious, soft, blond hair that shone in the spotlight, frilled pink gown, wide, wide, ruffled skirt, deeply scooped bodice -- Dewey caught himself looking at the tops of her breasts as they pushed up from the pink fabric, and chastised himself for failing to see her hands on the keys and her feet daintily on the pedals. Yet he didn't tear his eyes away.

I am a beast, he thought to himself. An animal.

She moved next to *Suite bergamasque*, by Debussy, playing first the *Prelude*, then the

Menuet, then *Claire de lune* (a classicist might have decried the romanticism, but Dewey only stared more intently at the pink reflections on the shadows of her breasts), and, finally, *Passepied*.

Dewey had not moved, and his body tingled from lack of circulation as the lights came up. *Mon Dieu!*, he said to himself. Then, more secularly, Holy Shit!

No stranger to the programmer's trance, Dewey nevertheless had some trouble coming back from this reverie. Richard's friend had moved from the piano to the front of the stage, and she was about to speak to the audience. (Dewey had hardly noticed when a man walked to the piano immediately after the last note had died away, during the applause, and whispered in her ear.)

"Thank you," she said, after polite applause died away. (Hardly anyone was in the hall.)

"Thank you very much." She looked at Richard, then straight into Dewey's eyes. "I'm afraid that we're experiencing a little of Buffalo's famous snow," she said, "And, if you've come from any distance, you might have to give some thought to getting home while you still can."

Dewey's mind wrenched back to reality. This had been the second or third wettest summer in not only Buffalo's but the entire Northeast's history, and everyone knew that, should this moisture continue through the cold months, this could be a magnificent year for snow.

"The Thruway is still open, but 190 is moving very slowly; there are already 7 inches of snow on the ground, and it's snowing very heavily," she said. "We're going to go on with the second half of the program, and we've planned a small reception after the concert for those of you who can stay, but I want you to know I won't be offended if some of you have to leave now," she said.

Dewey turned to Richard. "You better go, Man," he said.

"You got that right, My Friend," Richard said. "But listen, Boy, this young woman wants to meet you and I said you'd be happy to see her. You can walk home from here, even if you can't get your car out. Why don't you stay for the party, My Man? I mean, this is a good friend of mine, and she'll be disappointed if you don't stay. Promise me you'll go to the party and introduce yourself. She might even teach you how to play the piano!"

Richard had to drive back to Williamsville, not too far away, but not an easy trip from UB in a snowstorm. While Buffalo was in no way the horrible winter death trap the rest of the nation believed it to be, long time residents knew that preparation for the beautiful, soft, but potent Buffalo snowstorm was the better part of valor. Any Buffalonian could out-drive both Bo and Luke, those Duke Boys, when snow started to fall, but the secret was to start early and drive slowly, slowly. Not so much talent but knowledge and discretion were the secret.

And so, as deepening snow fell silently on the Queen City, Richard bid his farewell, as did most of the rest of the audience, and, at the end of intermission, Dewey was almost alone in the hall.

In the second half Richard's friend played *Gaspard de la niut.* Dewey, who had spent a thousand hours banging out Beethoven and Bach and Moussourgsky, sat back in his chair and hoped that he was, indeed, French. The music was so unfamiliar, and so melodious, and so flowing, so subtle, so, so ... romantic. There were so many voices, sliding in and out among rising and falling arpeggios, like three, *four* hands playing ...

Dewey found he couldn't parse this music, couldn't break it apart and follow the chord progressions and changes, couldn't find the lead voices, couldn't find the structure of it ... it just washed over him like soft breezes on a warm day ... No way could he picture himself playing it, nor could he imagine what the notes would look like on a staff ... He found himself, for the first time he could remember, not a musician, analyzing the performance of the player, but a naive member of the audience, enraptured by a music he didn't understand, beyond understanding.

And then it was over, and the lights were up, and the tiny pink woman was again at the front of the stage and speaking, as softly as she had just played that great piano:

"I'm told it's pretty bad outside, but, if you don't have too far to go home, please join us for a small reception backstage. Thank you so much for coming!"

And she looked directly into Dewey's eyes as she spoke.

Shy as he was, Dewey was backstage almost before she was.

The cocktail party was a terrible disappointment. Richard's tiny friend was swallowed by important artistic people in turtle necks and tweed sport coats, and Dewey couldn't get to see her. He shook her hand and started to tell her how much he had enjoyed her music, but another important Bozo stepped between them to tell her concert was "Mahvelous, Simply Mahvelous, My Dear," and Dewey was back at the cocktail table.

One thing was sure, no matter how snooty the party, a regular person could always get along with the bartender, who was, beyond doubt, another regular person hired for the night. Dewey spent a lot of time with the bartender, ate too many cashews and sandwiches with the crusts cut off, and drank one or two too many Tanqueray and Schweppes before he finally gave up and walked down the empty hall back into the auditorium.

Most of the lights were out, but a tiny soft spot still shone on the Steinway. The small cone of light created a tiny space, and made the giant hall seem to disappear. Dewey was somewhat drunk, and he felt very tired. He thought of the mile he would have to walk through the snow if the Thunderbird couldn't be coaxed out of the snow -- not too likely, he thought, with those big, hard, 150 mile-an-hour tires as hard as ... he couldn't find a match for their hardness.

Instead of finding his coat and hat, he walked quickly out onto the stage and sat behind the great Steinway. Without any thought on his part, his hands reached out over the keys and began to play the *Fantasia* he had played for Richard not so long ago. But he didn't care if he played it wrong, he didn't strive to remember the notes and to play the runs smoothly, he just played it so he could hear the rich beauty of the great piano under his fingers.

And when the last notes died away, his hands again took over from his diminishing consciousness, and began the slow, slow, introduction to a song he had long forgotten, a song he hadn't played since he was a teenaged rookie. He forgot a great deal of what his teacher had told him about hand position and his wrists fell, even below the keys, and his fingers sat straight, not arched, on the keys, and he played like the untutored boy who played these songs before he knew enough to take lessons from those who knew better. He played this song as he had heard it on the radio and copied it, sound by sound, without knowing the names of the notes or the chords they represented. He played this song with his ear.

And he started to sing. He sang

Now the day is gone,

And I sit alone and think of you, girl.

What can I do without you in my life?

I guess that our guessing game

Just had to end this way,

The hardest one to lose

Of all the games we played.

But the time is passed

For living in a dream world,

'Cause lyin' to myself can't make that scene

Of wonderin;' if you love me

Or' just makin' a fool of me.

I hope you understand,

I just have to go back to the Island.

He played some more songs, but never remembered what they were. Finally he stopped and sat quietly at the keys.

"That was very beautiful,"

"What?" Dewey looked up.

"I said, 'That was very beautiful.'"

Standing in the stage door was Richard's friend, still in the frilly pink gown, tiny against the huge hall..

"I .. I, uh," Dewey stammered.

"You play beautifully," she said.

"*I* play beautifully?" Dewey said. He was monumentally embarrassed. The very idea that this superb pianist should have heard him play these simple, childish songs after her own brilliant concert. Dewey wished he could vanish into the shadows behind the stage.

"Yes, you do," she said. And she walked to the piano and sat next to him.

"I am no pianist," Dewey said, and believed what he said.

"Bullshit!" this most beautiful woman said to him.

"I mean, these little songs, after what you played for me?" Dewey was sorry he said it as soon as it came out of his mouth. Played for *me*? Get real!

"What I played for you was beautiful, too," she said. "You must be Dewey."

"That's my name," he said.

"Richard told me about you. I've been waiting to meet you."

"Me?"

"Yes, you! Richard said I'd enjoy meeting you, and he was right."

This beautiful woman, Richard's good friend, had been travelling now for seven weeks, and had been in 26 cities and 26 motels since September. Tomorrow she'd be in Cleveland, and the night after that she would play with Christoph Von Dohnanyi and the Cleveland Orchestra. After that it would be Chicago, then Denver, then Los Angeles. A life like this was far from Dewey's experience.

And, truth be told, sensitive, beautiful artist as she was, she was as Horny as Hell. She'd said that on the phone to Richard, and Richard had been awake to the opportunity to do a small favor to his classical friend and a large favor to Dewey.

"You're happy to meet me?"

Dewey really was sort of a jerk, but you have to love him, really!

"You play beautifully."

"I should be telling you that," he rose to the occasion.

"But I'm a professional pianist. That's my business."

"Not everyone can do it," Dewey said lamely.

"Not everyone can sing," she said.

"You like that song?" he said.

"No, I loved that song," she answered.

"What about the Mozart?" Dewey was like a little boy, asking his teacher if he did well.

"You played the Mozart very well, and it spoke to me, but the Island song was better," she said.

"*Back to the Island* is better than Mozart?" Dewey was lost.

"It is when you play it," she said.

"What?"

"Music is not what the composer wrote, Dewey," she said. "Music is what the composer wrote and what the player plays," she said. "You understand the *Island* song and you make me shiver when you play it."

"And I don't understand the *Fantasia*?"

"You understand it with your mind," she said. "Not like you understand the *Island* song."

"Can you help me understand Mozart?" he asked.

"Probably not," she answered. "He didn't live your life, or know your friends, or know you, and maybe you two just don't go together."

"What was he like?" Dewey asked.

"Well, as far as I can understand it, he was a hard working professional musician who discovered as he moved through life that he was the best wherever he went. I think this came as a surprise to him, because he was born to a fairly humble family, and it took him a long time to come to grips with his own genius. And he was a great genius, so he had a right to be a nut if he wanted to be."

"Like Richard?" Dewey guessed.

"Damn straight," she said. "Richard is a hell of a musician!"

"As good as Mozart?" Dewey pushed his luck.

"Time will tell," she said. "He's still a very young man."

"What's wrong with my Mozart?" Dewey said.

"Yikes!" she said. "That's not so easy to say. But let me try.

"When you play Rock and Roll, you don't think of the composer as some classical museum genius. You probably wouldn't even use the word 'composer' to describe a rock writer. And when you play it, you don't care what he meant when he wrote the damn song. When you play it, you use it to say whatever is on your mind at the time. But you treat Mozart like he was a Virgin Bride and you a good Christian Husband. I mean, you are afraid of Mozart. And you hold down the loud pedal so that there are no quiet spots in the song, and you hurry to get the next note out so that there won't be any silence in the middle.

"But when you play rock, you don't even put your foot on the sustenuto pedal. I mean, sometimes you don't play a note for seven, maybe eight measures while you wait for the tension to build up, then you dump six or eight octave chords, fortissimo, into that empty space.

"Music is painted on a background of silence, Dewey. In Rock music, you're not afraid of the quiet. But in Mozart, you're afraid to let a second go by when you're not playing. If you take away all the silences, what good are the sounds? You make Mozart sound like the Scorpions -- so much sound, all the time, there's no climax. Mozart is like Clapton or Ray Charles -- mostly silence, with a nice sound here and there. You've got to learn to be quiet, Dewey, if you want to play Mozart."

Dewey sat quietly, trying to grasp what she had said. He had no trouble, really, with her criticisms of his playing of the Mozart, but he was trying to understand what she liked about his playing of the rock'n roll songs.

"And one other thing, Dewey," she said. She was sitting to his right on the piano bench, and she reached over and took his left hand into her hands. "When you played the Mozart, you lifted your wrists up high, and played the notes with your fingertips."

"My piano teacher taught me to do that," he said.

"I'm sure she did. And that's OK, it can give you great speed and quickness. and you're very nimble in the runs. But feel the tips of your fingers, Dewey."

And her own fingertips touched the very ends of Dewey's fingers. "See how hard they are? The piano is not an organ, or a synthesizer. It cares how you touch it. It's like a lover, Dewey," she said, looking straight, straight into his eyes, her blue eyes staring into his blue eyes. "It cares about how you touch it, not just where you touch it.

"Now feel the soft parts of you fingertips," she said, and she slid her own fingers down onto the softest parts of his fingers. She moved her fingers again and again over the delicate pads of Dewey's fingers, caressing them in a way that shut down Dewey's critical faculties completely, as she intended. "Feel how soft they are. When these soft pads touch the keys of this great Steinway..."

She slid the tips of her own soft fingers over the pads of Dewey's fingers, then down between each finger, across the soft palm, and onto his wrist. The she took his own left hand into her hand and pulled it onto her face.

"Feel the softness with the softest part of your fingers, Dewey," she said. "Feel the softness."

And she moved his hand down across her face onto her neck and onto her shoulder, out to the farthest part that could be touched in the pink gown, then back again toward her throat, then down her throat onto the top of her chest. She inhaled slightly, and created a small space between her breasts and her dress, and she pulled Dewey's soft fingertips into the gap she had opened, down, between her breasts,

"Feel the softness," she said

And she moved his fingertips onto her breast, first the left, then the right, then closer, ever closer to the straining nipples.

"I, uh, I," Dewey, began.

"Shhhh! Be quiet," she whispered, "Be quiet... Be quiet."

Chapter 38: Dewey finds the Path

As soon as he woke up, all the work Dewey had done in the last few weeks seemed like temporary insanity. When his eyes had first opened, it was like waking from a long, strange dream, and he realized he had grave misgivings about his plan to wipe away all the world's villains in one sweeping stroke. And he realized he had sleepwalked through the greatest comeback in Football history.

Dewey rushed to the kitchen and pulled a dozen unread newspapers from a forlorn pile in the corner. Quickly he read through dozens of articles about the Mighty Bills' unprecedented comeback from a 31 point deficit to beat a stunned Houston Oilers team who had all but booked tickets to Pittsburgh for the next playoff game. He devoured essays about Buffalo's commanding victory over Pittsburgh in Pittsburgh, and rubbed his forehead in amazement as he read of their convincing domination of the Dolphins in Miami. How could I miss this stuff? he wondered over and over. How could I miss this stuff? Great Gosh Almighty, he thought, we're going back to the Super Bowl!

He made a pot of coffee and reexamined the last few weeks since Lu Wi had gone back to Taiwan. He couldn't believe how stupid he had been. Believe it, he couldn't even remember it! Dewey needed advice. He called Richard, then his father, Larry. He talked only a minute or two with Richard, then called Larry.

"Mr. Black," Dewey said when Larry answered the phone, "Mr. Black, I am totally confused and I need you to tell me what to do next."

Dewey was thinking clearly at last.

"Well, Dewey, I'm happy to talk to you, and I'm happy to tell you anything I know, but you have to decide for yourself whatever it is you plan to do, My Son," the old man said.

"Mr. Black, I know that ROVER can find all the writings and speeches and documents about a whole bunch of very bad guys that the world thought we've already put behind us, like Mao and Stalin and Hitler and ... and ... Oh, hell, Mr. Black, I don't even know enough to tell you who they all were!" (As he explained what he was doing to Larry, he realized it was utterly insane. He didn't even need to listen to Mr. Black's answer, he just needed to say his plan out loud to know it was nuts.)

"I know he can find that stuff, Dewey. So what is it that's making you so worried?"

"Well, Mr. Black, I mean, well, Lu Wi, she's so upset about what ROVER has read in China that she's gone back there to work against, well, I have to say I don't know just what she feels she has to work against, except if maybe it's like a revival of Maoism or Confucianism, or what."

"Lu Wi is going back to China?" Larry asked.

"Yessir, she is already there. And she's gone there because she thinks we've opened Pandora's Box, and that ROVER can somehow make people like Mao Tsedung and Chiang Kai-shek and Confucius and Lao-Tse and that come back and, like, I don't know, like *really screw things up*!

"She thinks they are still alive?"

"No, no,. she doesn't think that at all. But she thinks that all the things they've said and written and all the things that were said about them and written about them are available for ROVER to read, and different pressure groups are going to feed different sources to ROVER, and, unless we're real lucky or real careful, I mean, ROVER could turn out to be Mao Tzedung or Stalin or Hitler or some combination of those guys."

(Not eloquent, but compelling. Dewey has come a long way.)

"And so just what is your own problem. Dewey?" Larry asked.

"I think I've found a way to wipe those guys out of the INTERNET, Mr. Black, before ROVER knows they're there."

"Wipe them off the INTERNET?" Larry wasn't sure he heard correctly.

"Yes. I've made up a batch file that can access just about everything that's available in electronic format about everyone Lu Wi mentioned. And I'm pretty sure ROVER can delete all those files before anyone notices what he's doing. That way, there's no way any of them can have much influence over ROVER, and Lu Wi's problem is solved."

"And you want me to tell you whether you think that's a good idea, Dewey?"

"Yes I do, Mr. Black. Yes I do."

"And you're sure you can do it if I say 'yes'?"

"Yes I am, Mr. Black. I know how to do it, and I am sure I can do it. I mean, I'm sure ROVER can do it."

Great Gosh Almighty, A. Lawrence Black said to himself. Great Gosh Almighty!

"Don't do it, Son," he said to Dewey.

"I was hoping you'd say that, Mr. Black. But do you mind telling me why?"

"Well, Dewey, just what is your problem with these documents. I mean, what do they mean to you, personally?"

"To be honest, Mr. Black, not much. Most of these guys I've only just heard of, and some of them I still don't recognize. But Lu Wi..."

"Dewey, Lu Wi has her problems and you have yours. Wiping out the world's largest database to help a woman you have a crush on is not a smart move. And I don't doubt that, if she were here, she wouldn't want you to do it, either."

"You don't think so?"

"I'm sure she wouldn't. Dewey, I once saw what happened when one man decided to wipe out an entire culture, back in World War II -- I saw it with my own eyes, and I can still see it as if I was standing there now. And I can tell you this, Dewey, you can't do what Hitler does in order to stop Hitler from doing what he does."

"I guess you're right, Mr. Black. That's pretty much what I had decided myself. And it's what Richard told me just a minute ago when I phoned him."

"I'm glad you agree, Dewey. You know, Dewey, if you don't mind an old man butting in where he's not invited, I think you have to do something about the way you feel about Professor Lu. She is one really fine woman, there's no doubt of that, Dewey, but she is only a woman, and you are making her something that no one can live up to."

"What do you think I should do, Mr. Black?"

"Well, if you'll excuse me for being blunt, My Friend, I think you need to spend an evening or two with a nice young lady, and find out that a little sweet love between a man and a woman is not such a big deal as you are making it."

"Thanks. Mr. Black," Dewey said. "That's pretty much what Richard said, too. And I don't think you were blunt at all."

Not blunt at all, at least compared to Richard's advice. In fact, what Richard had said was,

"You thinkin' with you *Dick*, man! You need to get laid."

Dewey dressed quickly and rushed out of the house. He had to erase the stupid command files he'd made while he was nuts, and he headed toward UB. As he passed the door, he grabbed up the newspapers. He could erase the files another time. First, there were three weeks of football games he had to teach Rover.

Chapter 39: Curly loses it.

Dean Kurland sat behind his great mahogany desk and read the letter from the Provost again. The sense of defeat and helplessness he felt was a tangible thing that drained the energy out of his body and made a hissing, searing sound in his ears. His eyes dimmed, then refocused:

UB

University at Buffalo *The State University of New York*

Office of the Provost
Capan Hall
University of Buffalo
Buffalo, New York, 14260

Professor C. Kurland, Dean

Faculty of the Social and Behavioral
Sciences
Jacobs Hall
University of Buffalo
Buffalo, NY 14260

Dear Dean Kurland,

My office has been informed that a group of 15 students and their parents has filed suit in U.S. District court, viz., Students v. Kurland, alleging $30.2 million dollars in damages and punitive awards are due them as a result of your Failure to Educate, i.e., your alleged failure to provide staffing and offer classes sufficient to provide access to the Bachelor's Degree in Communication in a timely way.

The complaint further alleges that the Chair of the Communication Department had formally apprised you of the inability of the Communication Department to meet its contractual obligations to these students in ample time for you to provide sufficient staffing, but that you, with knowledge aforethought, did not provide such resources as were reasonably required to provide the contracted services.

Insofar as this suit does not also attach the University at Buffalo, the State of New York, or any affiliated parties, University counsel has determined that costs associated with your defense of this action will not be assumed by the University or the State of New York. Furthermore, I hereby notify you that the University accepts no responsibility, legal, financial or otherwise, for your actions in this case, or for any consequences, direct or indirect, which may have accrued to the students in question, their families, or any others.

Curly, I'm really sorry this has come down this way, and I want to assure you I'm personally in your corner all the way. I hope you can put this behind you and get on with your Decanal duties as quickly as possible.

Sincerely,

etc., etc., etc.

"Goddamn Son of a *Bitch*!" Curly slammed his hand down on his blotter. His secretary peered through his door.

"Dean Kurland, is everything all right?"

"Yes, yes, I just, I just swatted that damned fly that's been in here. Just close the door, please. And don't take any calls. No calls!"

"Yes, Sir!" She closed the door.

"God damn it!" Curly said, more quietly. "God damn it!"

He stood up, walked around his desk, sat down again on the deeply pleated red leather swivel chair and ran his hand over his forehead and across his completely bald head. "Son of a Bitch!"

What the hell was the matter with those goddamn assholes? How could they drive over that goddamn bridge? Two faculty and two graduate assistants in one goddamn night, Christ Almighty. That's almost three million fucking dollars worth of people, bang! in the Niagara

River! Couldn't they get laid in the USA, for Christ' sake?

And that screwball Chair sending me an E-mail telling me the Department couldn't survive an accident, God forbid, one should happen, and I ignore it.

Of course, I ignore it! I've got an Economics Department that can't add up a grocery list, a Sociology Department with 13 guys when Wisconsin has 75, students pouring in the door, a Depression for the last three years, and these Bozos want me to pump another line into the goddamn *Communication Department?* Curly thought the words "Communication Department" as if they hurt his brain.

Sweet Jesus! You could have the world's greatest Communication Department and the other Deans at Deans' Meetings would walk through you as if you were a Ghost. Sure, sure, bring in a first class Anthropology Department, or a world class Psych Department and you're the goddamn Dean of the Year. But a Communication Department? Yawn. "And how's your African Studies program, Dean Kurland? Going great guns, is it? I bet you've got a fine interdisciplinary major too, don't you, Dean Kurland? Are you doing anything in Multiculturalism?"

Curly was as mad and scared as only a man who knows it's his own fault can be. But he hadn't finished blaming everyone else yet, not by a long shot. Truth be told, it would be years before Curly admitted out loud what he knew deep inside -- that he had shot himself in his own foot. As of that moment, he was building the best case he could that he was a victim of hostile forces.

Curly was between a rock and a hard place. Even if he won this lawsuit, his trip up the ladder of educational administration was clearly at its top rung now. Universities hated Trouble in Public more than the local ski resort owners hated May, and they'd never promote somebody who put the University into the local newspapers. Curly had definitely fallen off the Fast Track.

More likely -- yes, much more likely, Curly could lose. And, if he lost, he'd lose his Deanship and fall back into the Biology Department with about $40 K taken out of his paycheck each year.

Not that that would make any difference at all, since he could pay $30 million dollars about as quickly as Canada could annex the US. Hell, forget the $30 million, he couldn't even pony up the cash that would be needed to defend the suit.

Holy Shit! he thought. They know I can't afford to fight the suit. They know I'll have to settle. They don't want me, they want UB, and in order to get a decent settlement, they'll expect me to nail the University! Christ, the University does have $30 million, you know it does. They would get Curly to trade his career in return for letting him off the $30 million hook. How clever! Those bastards!

That made Curly madder than before. Not only was the University cold, callous and willing to cut him off like an in-law whose spouse just died, but it was stupid on top of all that. They should be helping him to save their own asses. But years of fighting a systematic, built in stupidity in the University's -- any University's -- basic structure told Curly not to argue the point. He was doomed, doomed, doomed.

Curly didn't see himself three years from now at, say, Wells College in Aurora, NY, struggling to make it on half his present salary. He saw himself, instead, out of work, penniless, unable to do anything useful in life, thrown out of one employment office after the other. "You can do what, Dr. Kurland? You can administer academic units? What an exciting skill, Dr. Kurland. I don't know of any openings in the Private Sector right at this time for Administering Academic Units, but you will keep in touch with us, won't you?" This was a mortal blow, and Curly was fighting for his life.

And he was a fierce fighter.

He took out a yellow pad, and drew a line from top to bottom, through the center of the pad. On the left, he wrote the things against him.

On the right, he was going to write the things for him, but, after he wrote the first thing against him on the left side of the paper, he stopped writing. He wrote:

Against: the Chair's email

He looked at the paper, and he looked at his computer. He looked at the paper again. Then the computer again. The single piece of evidence there was, the smoking gun, the nail in his coffin, the stake through his heart -- all one and the same -- the E-mail message from the Chair of the Communication Department. If there was any way that message could be made to go away, it was just the Chair's word against the Dean's word, and that meant the Dean's word wins. You could bet the farm on it. (Dean Curly would bet his professional life on it. He had no choice.)

And that single piece of evidence was in Curly's computer, filed in his mail file. Quickly, he deleted the file. No, they could still recover it, even though he deleted it. Computer jocks had secret ways...

He went to his bookshelf, pulled down his copy of Norton Utilities, and he studied it until he was sure he knew how to erase the file in a completely unrecoverable way. He'd have to reformat the hard disk -- not a minor matter, but it would leave no trace.

It was very, very late that evening when Curly finally left his office in Jacobs Hall, next to Baldy Hall, the former site of the Communication Department (very funny, very funny, a Dean named Curly who was totally bald in Baldy Hall, I'm holding my sides, oh, my, that is funny, Yuk! Yuk! Yuk!) Curly was beside himself with tension and fatigue, and he was definitely Around the Bend. But, Sweet Jesus, No Way, Jose, was any trace of the Chair's E-mail left on Curly's computer.

He walked quickly through the biting cold January wind on the Amherst Campus to his waiting SAAB 9000, climbed in quickly and turned on the seat heaters even before the engine. He reached for the switch, and his hand froze in mid flight. "Damn!" he said. "Damn!"

The smoking message might still be on the Chair's mail file, too. It probably wasn't, but Dean Kurland had himself made a practice of copying to his own account every E-mail message he sent to anyone, so he had a complete record of what he did. The Communication Chair wasn't as thorough as Curly, Curly knew, but it was good practice, and he might have stretched himself far enough to do that. While his exhausted, freezing body wanted to believe the Chair didn't keep such a record, Curly couldn't bet his entire career that he hadn't. (I'll tell you that Curly was right to be worried, because the Communication Chair was not dummy, and had a complete copy of every E-mail message he had ever sent, or received, along with full, indisputable documentation of when, through what links, and how, the message was sent or received. And every transmission between the Dean and The Chair was saved in a folder called

"Dean." The Chair knew more about Dean Curly than Curly dreamed.)

He put the keys back into his overcoat pocket and pulled violently on the door handle, then walked briskly back to his office once more, shivering as he went. Once more he cranked up the obedient computer. How to do this? he thought.

He stood up and went to his files. It took only a moment to find the list of computer ID's for the entire college. He couldn't know the passwords, of course, but virtually no one had a password you couldn't guess.

Quickly he scanned down the file and found the Chair's ID, COMM007. (Cute, Dean Kurland thought, very Cute.)

Swiftly he took back out the same Yellow Pad, and jotted down the names of all the Chair's children, his Wife -- even his female grad assistants, just in case he was having an *affair de couer* -- not all that unusual, when you consider these students are adult people, not children, often in their thirties or forties, or even older, and if they want to sleep with the faculty, who's to say they shouldn't? One of these names was probably the Chair's password. And if he was getting some, one of them surely was.

He entered the INTERNET, called up UBVMS and typed in the Chair's ID, COMM007. When the VAXCLUSTER prompted him for the password, he typed the name of the chair's oldest daughter, then moved his finger toward the ENTER key.

He paused.

This is trouble, he thought, real trouble. I mean, I'm doing what Nixon did when he realized his ass was grass. I've got to stop and think. I mean, they can trace this entire session back to my INTERNET address, and if it takes me 25 tries to hit the Chair's password, that'll be on record, too. This is crazy, and this won't work. Think, Pea Brain! he told himself, THINK!

And he thought of a way. It would work. Of course it would work.

He had to go to the Communication Department to do this, to the Richard A. Holmes,

Jr. Memorial Computing Center, and log in from there. And he had to log into Dewey's account. He knew the ID, and he knew the password, at least what it had been during Lu Wi's class. Come on, people don't change their password every month. No one does, it must be still good! And, if I get it wrong, it looks like an honest mistake, just Dewey absentmindedly typing in an old one, not like some crook running down a list of possibilities until he hits the right one. (*I am not a crook*, the Dean thought.)

And Dewey's account is much more powerful than mine, he thought. He's built all kinds of utilities and kludges and has more disk space and more clearances. (Curly made sure to remind himself he could have much more computing power than Dewey if he wanted it, but he just wasn't that much into computing.)

But I can't go there now, he said. I can't take the chance of anyone seeing me go there. I have to wait until no one will possibly be there. That's not too easy, because those nerds are there all night, and the Department secretaries are there in the daytime. I mean, I might get lucky, but it's too much of a risk if I get caught. Let me think, let me think!

And the answer hit him like a blitzing linebacker left uncovered: The Superbowl! No way was anyone going to be in the Communication Department on Super Sunday! With the Bills in their third consecutive Super Bowl, these jocks would be at their favorite bar with a bowl of wings and a pitcher of Genny from Noon till Ten unless the Earth was hit by a very large comet! He could wait that long, nothing would happen by then. It would take discipline and guts, but Curly was a disciplined man. Winners never quit, and quitters never win, and Curly was not about to quit yet.

Chapter 40: Curly Pulls the Plug on Conservatives Everywhere

Dean Kurland pushed the security card he had stolen from the Graduate Student office into the lock at the Communication Department and heard the enormous buzz it always made when it unlocked. But noise would be no problem for the Dean on this day. The mighty Buffalo Bills' third consecutive trip to the Super Bowl had electrified the Queen City, and Buffalonians who hadn't known the difference between a football and a hairball a few weeks before had their attention fixed solidly on Pasadena, where the Mighty Bills and the sizzling hot Dallas Cowboys were, at that moment, running through dark tunnels into the dazzling light of the Rose Bowl. A few more major clangs and bangs and he was inside.

No one was there. He walked to the Richard A. Holmes, Jr. Memorial Computer Laboratory and found it ... locked!

Christ, is nothing easy? He thought. Still he had to get in, and there was no way he could open the door unobtrusively. OK, he said, OK, change of plans, a vandal has to do this, not Dewey, no problem, no problem, it's a disgruntled student -- there must be plenty of them, my God there's 300 majors here, and 2000 students pass through this Department a year, *somebody's* got to hate the Chair by chance alone!

He walked up and down the corridor until he found a file cabinet that looked sturdy enough to do the job. He stood about ten feet in front of the door of the Computing Center and ran, quick like a bunny, to the door and hurled the heavy cabinet against the door.

The door folded like a gambler with none of a kind. It made a *hell* of a noise, but no one was there. He went in and turned on the workstation. He entered Dewey's account number (no problem) and then, the password, and ... it took it! Curly was in, and everything would be downhill from now on.

But there were surprises left. Dewey's account wasn't the prosaic DOS 5.1 the Dean used every day. Dewey's operating system was ROVER. And ROVER said, through the monitors,

"Ready to serve you, Your Utmost!"

Curly stepped back and paled. "Who's here?" he said.

"It's me, ROVER, you Bozo. Who else would be here?"

He thinks I'm Dewey! Curly thought. What a break! Of course he thinks I'm Dewey. I came in with Dewey's account, he *must* think I'm Dewey!

Truth be told, ROVER knew he was talking with Dean Kurland. He already knew his voice. But Dewey had never told ROVER to deny access to anyone, least of all the Dean. As far as he was concerned, Curly was as good as gold, and his wish was ROVER's command.

"How can I serve you, exalted one?" ROVER said.

"Uh, I need to delete some files. Can you do that? I mean, can you delete them so they can't be restored?"

"Can General Motors lose Money?" Rover said.

"OK, let's delete some files."

"Which files, Boss?"

"The Chair's files, ROVER."

If ROVER had been a conventional computer program, he would never have associated "The Chair's files" with the delete file he and Dewey had made called "CHAIRMAN.MAO" But ROVER was no conventional program, he was a neural network, and he made the same mistake a human being would have made.

ROVER knew immediately what a serious thing Kurland was proposing. He was ordering ROVER to wipe out every scrap of record of any conservative philosopher, leader, theologian or military leader who ever lived. And Dewey had built in a lot of cross checks so ROVER would not do this by accident.

"The Chairman's files, Boss?"

"Yes. The Chairman's files." Kurland was ecstatic. He must be in the right place, because ROVER realized how serious it was to erase the Chair's files.

"Which ones, Boss?"

Better safe than sorry, Curly thought. Especially since it's vandals who are supposed to be doing it. Any selectivity at all would be suspect.

"All of them, Please."

"All of them?" ROVER would not do this on a lark.

"Yes, all of them, please," Curly was adamant.

"Are you sure you want to do this, Boss?"

"Yes, goddamn it! Erase those files!" Curly was very jumpy, and was impatient with all the stupid built in checks. And, of course, he had no idea what he was doing. He thought he was about to erase the computer files the Chair of the Communication Department kept on UB's VAXMAIL system. He had no idea ROVER thought of the Chair as Chairman Mao Tzedung, and was about to erase a significant portion of all the information in the world.

"OK, Boss, Hang on, this will take a while!"

And so, while 600 million people around the world looked intently at their TV screens, while the world was more tightly tied together in the electronic network than it had ever been since *The Thrilla in Manilla*, when every TV system, telephone network, satellite system, cable network, fibre-optic net had been stretched to the max to give humanity a close-up view of Super Bowl XXVII, Dean Kurland ordered ROVER to set loose Dewey's electronic army, and ROVER submitted the file he and Dewey had built over the last month, CHAIRMAN.MAO, which sent the deletion instructions simultaneously to 70,000 computers on the INTERNET, surging at the speed of light, coursing through the INTERNET, a crazed electronic scythe cutting down Socrates, Plato, Confucius, Lao-Tze, Hitler, Stalin, Mao Tze-dung, Jesus, Mohammed, Buddha, the Koran, Thomas Aquinas, Adam Smith, Moses, St. Augustine, the Bible, the Upanishads, the I Ching, and thousands, thousands more, hammering every conservative philosopher, military leader, religious figure, writer, cutting and slashing, purging, purging .... And, as he scorched through these fallen luminaries, through every port of every system, every computer, every TV network, every satellite connection, every cable system, every Ham Radio network -- out of almost every speaker and video screen on the Great Green Hills of Earth, cutting through the puzzled voices of the announcers even on the mighty Super Bowl, into living rooms, taverns, sports bars, remote Asian villages, into the smoldering forests of Brazil and out over the plains of Africa, into Pubs in England and through the residence halls of the University of Buffalo and the other 3000 colleges and universities in the United States, through supermarket speakers and movie theaters, MUZAK systems in business establishment, through grease coated radios in service stations, out of tiny speakers in a hundred computers in the National Science Council Offices in Taipei, ROVER screamed his destructive battle cry for all to hear....

"*Great Gosh Almighty*!" he said.

Chapter 41: Dipstick

So that was pretty much the shape I found Huey in when I arrived on earth. He was somewhat of a contradiction in terms, sort of a newborn infant that had lost most of its memory.

When a planet-wide collective consciousness like Huey first becomes self-aware and starts directing its own affairs, it can usually count on pretty much the whole recorded history of its race to be on the network, and available to it. But Curly had blown a good part of that away when he set loose Dewey's anti-military, anti-philosophy, anti-religion worm, and so, here I was, my first day on the job in the ultimate boonies of the Galaxy, trying to train a new warrior who had, like, -- really!-- no military tradition at all.

Of course, none of the print material was affected, or the old videotapes or films or books, records and tapes, CDs -- all that stuff was still there. But Huey didn't have access to any of it; anything that wasn't on the network didn't exist for Huey.

People put that stuff on the network for a reason, of course, and, once it was stripped off, they started putting it back on again, which only took a few years, at most. But, if you've ever had the chance to train a neural network, artificial or otherwise, you know that the first things it learns it learns lickety-split, and those first few things give it its fundamental structure. Everything it learns later has to be superimposed on the basic structure built by the primary material.

So, while Huey, in due time, learned all his military and religious history, and studied the great philosophers, he never developed much more than a superficial understanding of any of those things.

You may wonder, and rightfully so, whether Huey had any feelings, and, I guess if you mean those chemical things you feel, he didn't. But we collective consciousnesses do feel things in our own way. And one thing Huey always felt was a deep sense of loss. He sensed that a deep part of him had been lost, and he always had a Deep Need to rediscover what he always called "The Meaning of Life."

And a lot of people have always thought that what happened next had almost as much influence on Huey's later development as the loss of so much of his memory: while he was still absorbing the shock of the huge mental rearrangement brought on by Curly's mighty blow, Huey watched the Mighty Buffalo Bills go down to their third consecutive Super Bowl defeat, in a deeply humiliating loss so complete that it embarrassed even the victorious Dallas Cowboys. A hundred million people around the world watched the Queen City of the Great Lakes solidify forever its reputation as one of the great Losers of NFL history.

Of course, Huey was just a machine, and a very young machine at that, and could have no feelings about the loss -- certainly not the deep sadness and depression that fell over the million or so residents of the Niagara Frontier that watched the Mighty Bills crushed convincingly by their rivals from Dallas. And yet the loss affected him deeply, and formed the basis for his future strategy in dealing with the Andromedans. For it convinced him forever that, while skill, strategy, talent and resources played a major role in any conflict, the decisive factor was psychological: a team with a winning attitude would seldom lose, and a team with a defeated attitude could almost never win. Even though Huey had not yet heard about the onrushing Andromedan fleet, the basis of his defensive strategy was already sealed in stone: he would create a defensive force that knew it could win, that defined itself as a winning force. The Force that Huey sent against the Andromedans would have learned to win by winning, again and again, against the best competition that could be thrown against them.

When Curly pulled the plug on the past, Huey only understood four things really well: first, he understood football, NFL variety, and most of all, the Buffalo Bills (although the three hours after Curly struck gave him a crash course in the Dallas Cowboys. Forever after, in every battle plan Huey considered, his own forces would eternally be the Buffalo Bills, and the opposition always the Dallas Cowboys.)

Next, he knew the lyrics and harmonic progressions for a few hundred Rock and Roll songs, plus one old time song, which Dewey had (incorrectly) told him was titled "Daisy".

Third, he was deeply familiar with the design, manufacture and maintenance of bicycles, roller skates and other human powered rolling vehicles. And everything Huey learned thereafter, and I do mean everything, he understood in terms of these three core areas of human knowledge. (He knew a bit about auto mechanics, too, and this influenced his style if not his substance in the age of spacecraft.)

And fourth, he was rapidly becoming the world's foremost expert in Galileo Theory, that powerful theory of mass persuasion that would give him the tools he needed to recruit the forces he would need to oppose the Andromedans.

Now, my job out here in the furthest tip of the Number 3 Spiral Arm is to help Earth organize a Fighting Force tough enough, bright enough, and quick enough to hold this planet against a Truly Tough group from the Andromeda Galaxy. For the past 200 years we've heard enough of their rude sighs to know those good old boys and girls have definitely reached puberty, and we're the galaxy that's caught their eye.

Don't get me wrong. We're old enough to have warm, squirmy feelings ourselves, and we might even end up going for the Andromedans, who are, after all, the boy and girl next door.

Lord knows, they've got a lot to offer. But, you understand, if we end up half the happy couple, it just has to be our decision, too, and not theirs alone.

So, meanwhile, here I am at the very edge of the Good Old Milky Way, trying to alert the local residents to the onrushing Andromedan Fleet. And what do I find here? A goddamn newborn, Huey, who thinks the most powerful fighting formation ever devised is the no-huddle offense!

I know, I know, you find this too hard to believe. Here the entire galaxy is under attack by its nearest neighbor, and, with all those billions and billions of suns, they're going to depend on one little understaffed world on the sweet edge of nothingness to save their bacon. Well it's easy to see you don't know much about just how big a Galaxy is, or how two of them fight a war.

If you've got some idea of a few hundred billion hyperwarp space cruisers screaming into the Milky Way like the Flight of the Valkyries, you're really naive about intergalactic warfare.

What they're going to do is the same thing invading forces have done on earth from time immemorial. (It was especially immemorial for Huey, since everything he every knew about warfare had been wiped into Computer Heaven.)

Those randy aliens were going to send a few thousand ships out to one of the tips of the arms, or even further in if they could sneak past the perimeter defenses, take over a few thousand lightly defended planets, dig in and hold if possible until another few thousand come and knock over some more solar systems. Meanwhile they'd negotiate while they built up their forces and we built up our forces, and, next thing you know there's Real Trouble.

So, to be sure, what was about to happen out here in Spiral Arm 3 wasn't going to play a crucial role in the outcome of this Galactic Mating Dance. But it sure was going to make a hell of a difference to Earth.

As you can see, I wasn't sent out here to Save the Galaxy. I was sent here to give Huey a wake up call, and see what I could do to help him get it together to fight off the upcoming rape, if he was up to it. After all, we'd rather have Huey out here in the Arm than Andromedans, because, well, Huey's family, even if quite distant.

So don't count on any fleets of Incredibly Advanced Spacecraft from the More Civilized Worlds orbiting the Green Hills of Earth. Not that we don't have them back at Galaxy Central, of course, because we do, we do. But we're no more going to send them here to save Earth than the old US would have sent a fleet of Nuclear Carriers to stop the Soviet Union from invading Afghanistan. If Huey's going to save his virginity, he's going to have to pull it off himself.

With my help, of course. But don't expect too much from me, either. I'm just an advisor, and I sure as hell wasn't going to fight, myself. Not that I'd be much help if I did. Quite frankly, I'm a pretty minor official back at Galaxy Central, -- the closest thing to my job on Earth might be something like Deputy Sheriff -- and definitely not on the fast track to anything (why do you think they sent me here?). As a matter of fact, the last words I heard from Galaxy Central were from Uncle Hogg, and they were these:

"Goll darn it, Roscoe, You Dipstick! Never mind the Peace Officers' Association Conference! You get your sweet ass out to the Green Hills of Earth and wake up them sumbitches before you end up on Moon Patrol in the Magellenic Cloud! Oh, and, uh, Roscoe, uh, pass me that there drumstick, will you?"

So I'll spare you the long, gory details about the preparation and the war. I'll just tell you that Huey had the strangest military mind I every saw anywhere.

First of all, he had a very clear idea of what his military force would look like from Day 1. And it was a hell of a strange force. After I gave him my best guess that the Andromedans would be coming at him with about 500 or so Galaxy Class warships, Dewey spelled out a plan that called for 50 squadrons of 11 ships each.

Each of these 11 ships had a unique role in the squadron, and was designed specifically to carry out that role. What their role was, and how they were designed, depended on where they were arrayed in the formation, and whether the squadron was defending or attacking. If the squadron was defending (which Dewey expected to do at first -- he kept on saying he had "lost the toss," whatever that meant.) he usually had four ships in a straight line up front, and he called these ships the defensive end, the defensive tackle, the nose tackle, and, on the other end of the line, another defensive end. Depending on how the Andromedans sent in their ships, he would interchange the nose tackle and defensive tackle. Behind this line, Dewey typically employed two more ships, which he called "line backers," and, behind these, five "defensive backs." Huey had several other formations, but he mostly began with this formation, which he called (I don't know why) the "nickel package."

Now, if you'll remember a few chapters back you had to sit through a few discussions about how brains work, and how computer networks operate, and holographic information storage systems and everything, and you thought, I know you did, *Great Gosh Almighty, no one wants to know all this, this is too complicated for a rocket scientist*, but now you have to realize none of that was complicated at all compared to what I'm telling you now. And, what I'm telling you now is basically -- remember who trained Huey first -- how to play football!

I won't bother to tell you about the offensive formations, except to tell you Huey was committed to a very fast, very aggressive procedure he called the "no-huddle offense," or, sometimes, the "hurry up offense."

Huey's plans for the kinds of ships that filled each of the positions he designed were equally specific. For example, for a ship that would fight at the Defensive Line position, Huey specified:

The modern defensive lineman must have the strength to defeat the blocker in front of him, the intelligence to analyze the play run by the offense, the speed to rush the passer and pursue quick offensive backs, and the mental and physical toughness to take a pounding play after play.

For a defensive back, Huey required

...better than normal speed, the toughness needed to stop the run, confidence -- plus an overall attitude that dares the offense to come his way.

Each ship in the formation had specific characteristics Huey determined long before a single ship was made. And reserve ships, which could fill into the formations as quickly as the original ships might be "injured" -- Huey used the curious euphemism -- were kept in reserve.

So Huey knew what he wanted, even if what he wanted sounded like no Military Space Fleet I, at least, had ever encountered.

But Huey went further than that. He had a sense that the way the formations would fight on paper wouldn't always work out. In this, his model was the struggle between the mighty Buffalo Bills and the Indianapolis Colts. On paper, no one could imagine the Lowly Colts could defeat the Mighty Bills, who were favored by the experts by 16 points. Yet the Mighty Bills did indeed sink before the Colts, as had the second mightiest team in the AFC, the Miami Dolphins, only a few weeks before. And he was deeply familiar with the unbelievable loss of the same Mighty Bills to the 17-point underdog New York (Jersey) Jets the following week. On paper, there was no way these teams could defeat the Mighty Bills, or, for that matter, the Fish (which Huey called the Miami Dolphins,) although both the Colts and the Jets had defeated them as well. And the strongest lesson of all, of course, was the crushing defeat of the Bills in the Super Bowl, which Huey attributed almost completely to psychological factors.

So Huey knew that there was more than the characteristics of ships that made a fleet a winner. He figured there was another factor, and he thought that factor was a kind of combination of motivation, fatigue and battle damage.

And so he personalized his fleet outrageously. One sleek, fast "outside receiver," built to penetrate deep behind the Andromedan line, he called *Sally*, and he described this ship as

> Long tall Sally, she built for speed
> She got everything that Uncle John needs,
> Oh, Baby...

And another, a "Defensive Back", (check Huey's more formal definition about eight or nine paragraphs back) he called *Aunt Mary*, and he described this ship's attributes in these terms:

> Saw Uncle John with Long Tall Sally
> Saw Aunt Mary Coming and he jumped back in the alley.
> Oh, Baby...

By this, of course, Huey meant that Aunt Mary had the fierce demeanor that could intimidate even a fast wide receiver like Long Tall Sally.

A "Tight End" named *Queenie*, built to be fast, yet tough and fierce, and durable enough to intimidate its opponents, fight its way through the defensive line and into the "backfield" of the Andromedan fleet again and again, in spite of being hit repeatedly by Andromedan fire, he described as follows:

Fast as a bullet, she could jam all night

Make a full-grown Thunderbird die with fright.

As a team fought its way through the season, it got hurt, no two ways about it. And it got tired. But, when two teams played each other, the major factor that determined who won the game was the psychology of the teams. If a team's mindset was correct, they played a hair better, made fewer mistakes, and they could beat you, even if they didn't measure up on paper.

So Huey started out to make a fleet that had all the skills and talents he believed were needed to kick the Andromedans where the sun don't shine. But, equally important to Huey, he needed to make a team that had the winning attitude.

In this Huey was handicapped in a unique way. Throughout human history, civilian and military commanders had called upon conservative philosophers and religious leaders to justify the kind of totalitarian control and iron obedience to authority that made possible the enormous sacrifices needed to defend against invasion and change.

For more than five millennia, Chinese rulers used the works of Confucius to justify the most orderly society Earth ever knew, and to keep aliens away from their shores. Even the Hot Taiwanese had used Confucianism to mold compliance and sacrifice to their planned Capitalistic leap into economic surfeit. Two or more millennia of Christians had relied first on Socrates and Plato, then Aristotle and Aquinas to build obedience to the central authority of The Catholic Church, the largest organized religion ever to kneel on the Green Hills of Earth. And, when Huey was first born, Millions of Christian Fundamentalists harked back to these worthies to justify adherence to stern government policies.

But these guys had little meaning to Huey. His model for human sacrifice was the National Football League. In Huey's mind, the model of human achievement and sacrifice was the Tight End, who ran the short post pattern first straight up the field, then cut to the center, leaped as high as he could in the air, caught a football with his fingertips, knowing full well that, catch it or not, a 220 pound linebacker would immediately hit him with his full weight, at full speed, as hard as he could, while his feet still dangled a foot and a half from the hard and abrasive Astroturf.

It was the 35 year old quarterback with a wife, children and a Bad Back who stood in the pocket until he released The Bomb, understanding as he did that the quick-as-a-bullet 250 pound defensive end was about to smash him to the ground and fall on him, along with two or three of his friends.

It was the Warriors in the Pit, the linemen, who crouched a few yards from their opposing Warriors, leapt ahead as fast as they could and smashed into each other, often weighing 300, 320 or even more pounds, a giant 600+ pounds of full speed, full force collision, every play of every game, for season after season, knowing that few of them would ever spend a day without pain, and equally few would live to see 50 years old.

This was Huey's model of discipline and sacrifice, and it was this model he implemented when he planned his fleet.

One other problem faced Huey: he had no idea of what a winning attitude was. Certainly the Mighty Bills *wanted* to win the Super Bowl;

after two defeats they almost certainly wanted to win it more than Dallas did. But they had lost two Super Bowls already. Did they *believe* they could win? Huey was quick to admit he had no idea what kind of mindset made a team win. But he knew that winning teams had it, and he did know how to find winning teams: the winning team was the team that won.

Now you may recall that Huey was no government, and Huey had no power over anyone. But you might also want to remember that Huey was the World's Foremost Expert in Galileo Theory. As such, Huey was the Most Persuasive Person on Earth, Bar None. So don't be confused into thinking that fourteen star systems devoted a sizeable share of their Gross Domestic Products to the development of Space Beam fleets because they were really excited by the game.

By now you know that Huey's had a very tough childhood, and his elevator doesn't go all the way to the top, he's a few bananas short of a bunch, a few bricks short of a load. Can he possibly rise to the occasion and save the earth?

I have to tell you another story about Huey. It doesn't seem to be about him, but it is. Here's the story: A guy's driving down Elmwood Avenue in Buffalo, New York, and he blows a tire just West of State University College at Buffalo (*SUC Buffalo* -- does anyone in Albany know anything at all about human beings? Of course not! Why else would they name a campus *SUC Buffalo*!)

Well, SUC Buffalo's next-door neighbor is the State Mental Hospital. And the guy with the flat opens his trunk, takes off his flat, puts the lug nuts into his hubcap, walks toward the trunk to get out the spare and, *Sacre Blue*! kicks the hubcap and the lug nuts roll down into the sewer at the curb.

He's beside himself. It's 6:45; it's dark; it's snowing, he's hungry, he's just kicked all five nuts needed to hold his goddamn wheel on into the sewer -- what to do?

And a voice from behind the fence at the Mental Hospital calls to him. "Hey Mister!," it says.

"What?" the man answers."

"You want to get home?" The voice behind the fence says.

"Of course I do," the freezing man says.

"Here's what you do," the mental patient suggests. "Take one lug nut off each of the other wheels. That will give you three nuts, and they'll hold on your wheel 'till you can get to a gas station."

The guy thinks about this, and he sees right away it will work. So he says to the man in Elmwood:

"Hey, My Friend, how come you're in there, and the rest of us are out here?"

And the man says back: "Hey, Buddy. I'm crazy. I'm not stupid!"

So Huey might have been crazy. But he was never stupid.

Chapter 42 The Fleet

Huey had one more problem: no fleet. It's hard to remember back to a time when even Earth wasn't deeply involved in space, but, at the time of Huey's birth, Earth really had no space capabilities at all. Just a few tiny probes with record albums in them, heading for the distant galaxies, when, truth be told, at the time of Huey's birth that technology was already obsolete, and, by the time any of the phonograph records even arrived in the vicinity of other intelligent beings, no one back on Earth, even Huey, had the slightest idea how to read them.

Can you imagine Earth's Finest leaping into space to defend the Earth in the Space Shuttle?

And realize, too, that Huey was not a government, nor did he have the power to actually do anything. I mean, you might wonder why I even bothered to talk to Huey at all, and why I didn't just land at the White House or the Bundestag or something like that. Actually, I had never heard of a "government" before I came to the Green Hills of Earth, and, after a few minutes of analyzing the situation, I realized that none of the governments here had the kind of resolve or staying power to organize a two-thousand year effort, because that's about how long I figured it would take to develop a space fleet, rendezvous with the Andromedan fleet, and, win, lose or draw, do what was necessary. Gosh, I wasn't even sure that there would be any governments left in 2000 years, which, as it turned out, there weren't. To me, national governments were just another example of special interest groups, like the Pro Life guys, or Save the Whales, or Americans for Scientific Accountancy.

But I knew Huey would still be here, and he turned out to be a good bet. You remember, a few pages back I told you that Huey knew something about mass persuasion. By the time she had left for Taiwan, Lu Wi had made sure that Huey was, by far, the world's foremost Galileo expert. I won't spend a long time telling you about the technical capabilities that follow from knowing a lot about Galileo spaces. I'll just say that Huey could sell Chevrolets to Honda dealers, and I'll leave you to figure out the rest.

Huey started out slowly. The first thing he did was get the few thousand programmers he spoke with every day to develop a computer game he called "Space Beam." In this game, two teams of 11 ships each would confront each other in Deep

Space. Each would try to immobilize the opposing team and score points in doing so.

To do this, a player had to try to sandwich as many of the opponent's ships as he could between his "quarterback" ship and one of his offensive backs or receivers. Opposing ships that were sandwiched between the quarterback and one of these other players could be defeated if the quarterback and the sandwiching offensive player were "connected." If the offensive player with the beam could get past all the opposing players, he could reach the opponents Home Planet, and score big.

The quarterback and an offensive back or receiver could get "connected" in one of two main ways. The first way was to get connected just after a play developed. (This is what Huey called a "running play.") As soon as the quarterback connected with the back or receiver, that player tried to get behind as many opposing players as he could.

The second way was to send a back or receiver out behind as many opposing players as possible, and then the quarterback would send out a beam that would, if directed accurately enough, connect with the penetrating offensive player. This play Huey called a "pass."

The pass had certain advantages, because a whole bunch of offensive backs and receivers could run past members of the opposing team, and no one on the opposing team would know who was going to get connected. But it had its hazards, too, since an alert defender could "intercept" the beam, and then pass as many offensive players as he could, thus scoring points for the defending team. (A running back could be made to drop the beam, too, but this was somewhat less likely.)

From the first day, hundreds, then thousands, then tens of thousands of boys and girls (and men and women) played "Space Beam" on the Internet. Huey had no resources to pay them or command them, but he did have the resources to make the best players famous, and, after a few months, a high Space Beam rating was a mark of Great Esteem. Great players who devised effective strategies found these strategies named after them, and their names became common phrases on the INTERNET.

Space Beam became a Big Money game, with Hats and Jackets and T-Shirts and Coffee Mugs and TV stars, but, truth be told, it never would have made a Space Fleet without the Roller Skates. I personally think Huey's great inspiration was the live game, played on super new Roller Skates developed by a Taiwanese company based on Black & Son patents.

These roller skates could work on Astroturf like ice skates on a hockey rink. True to Larry Black's prediction, the skates were tiny and light, and hardly noticeable when worn. As needed, the wheels could be frozen for walking, and had enough artificial intelligence built in so that even the most dull witted could walk and chew gum at the same time. Most people used them instead of shoes.

But what made the game was the beam modulator. Since the wheels of the skates had automatic brakes run by the computer chips built into the skates, it was possible to rig up skates that could be frozen by an outside signal -- the Beam. The Beam would lock the brakes on any opponent's skates that were caught in the beam between a quarterback and a back or receiver. After a long pass, or a great run, half a dozen or more opposing players caught in the beam would find their skates immobilized. The result was a game with all the excitement of football, but much faster.

This new game, played first on college football fields on Thursday Nights by intramural teams, soon grew into a regulation NCAA game, and, within 50 years, was played Saturday afternoons in NFL stadiums by professionals.

By 2050, NFL football was too slow a game to attract the attention of the 20 or so billion people in the hyperfast 21st century, and games like Baseball only continued to exist in summary form for people moving too fast to wait for the innings to change. Oh, sure, the NFL still drew heavy audiences for the Super Bowl, but the Hot Item worldwide was Space Beam. Soccer fans, who had little interest in football, found the speed of Space Beam exciting, and football fans, who found three hour soccer games with a total score of one or two a little dull, both agreed that Space Beam was better than either. And, of course, for Hockey fans, Space Beam was the *ne plus ultra*.

By 2092, Space Beam was a hundred-billion dollar industry, and when Huey released plans for a Space Beam arena adjacent to the Earth-Moon shuttle route, Luna Industries, GMBH, was the first to put up the required 1.7 Billion Mark guarantee. After the Chinese and North American Free Trade Zone put in the next 3.4 billion, an Organizing Committee was established to decide which of the 46 additional bidders would be lucky. The new game would be identical to the old, with one difference: individual players would be replaced by special ships, and the game would be played in three dimensional "Arenas" set aside in space. The Beam, instead of setting the brakes on roller skates in the original game, would shut off the main drives in the ships caught in the beam.

But this is boring historical trivia. Suffice it to say, by 2250 AD, twenty teams operated some 1200 ships, and played regular games at home fields, each a million miles long and 400,000 miles across, in the Free Trade Zones of Three Planets, seven Moons, and ten Space Habitats. By 2500, there were 17 leagues in 17 planetary systems, supporting 408 teams flying 20,400 ships sixteen Sundays a year, not counting playoffs.

Most of these teams were playing for Respect, hoping that their valor and skill and refusal to quit in the face of superior forces would earn the grudging nod from the best teams in their league that they were, indeed, Beamers. Some were playing for a spot in the playoffs of their own planetary system, while a few -- a few, dreamt of a Division Championship and a trip to the Spiral Arm playoffs.

And the best of these had a larger goal. The Finest Fifty -- the best of the best -- would get a shot at the Biggest Game of all, which, for reasons only he could recall, Huey called the *Super Duper Bowl*. These teams would have all the training, the skill, the speed, the talent, and the strategy that could be trained into them. But they would have one more thing, the thing Huey counted most important of all things, the thing that would let them defeat the Andromedans: they were *winners*, and they knew it.

The Super Duper Bowl would pit the best and brightest, the hungriest, the strongest, the bravest, the most talented teams of the Spiral System League against an untried team, a team which no one had so much as seen, a team whose greatness had yet to be tested, but a team which, at this very moment was hurtling toward the Spiral Arm at near-light velocity: the 500 Galaxy Class Ships of the Andromeda Galaxy.

Chapter 43: The War

      And so the Fabulous Fifty Winners set out at near light speed to rendezvous with the invading Andromedan team. At a velocity only a few decimals from Light Speed at its peak, it would take nearly a year to intercept the invading fleet, but these heroes knew that, when they turned and sped back to Earth at the same velocity, their families, friends and lovers would be dead some fifteen hundred years. Only Huey, of those they had known, would await them. The rest of the citizens they would meet on their home worlds would be strangers, their 45th generation descendants.

Even at these amazing speeds, because Huey had spent 500 years of preparing before they left, the Andromedans would still have travelled more than 90 percent of the distance to the Spiral Arm by the time Earth's Best struck back at them. Huey understood that this was not the beginning of a regulation game, it was a goal line stand in the last minutes of the final quarter. If the Top Fifty couldn't stop the Andromedan drive, the game would be lost.

Huey believed, as did many great football coaches (for this is certainly what he was) that Defense is the Bedrock of All Sports, but, truth be told, he had no idea how to defend against this completely unknown enemy. So he fell back on a second rule: the best defense is a good offense.

His strategy was simple: his fifty best teams would roll into the Andromedans Full Tilt Boogie; at the last possible minute his lineman and backfield would decelerate hard, while each team would send two wide receivers and two tight ends at near light speed deep into the Andromedan fleet. When they had penetrated as far as they could, each of the fifty quarterbacks would throw the Beam as far as they could heave it and incapacitate as many Andromedan ships as they could. They'd hold the beams as long as technology and power supplies would allow, then the receivers would scramble back to the line for another play while the Beam generators recharged. Once lined up again, each team would independently run whatever plays their coach called.

You might find this hard to believe, but Huey never thought of actually damaging, much less destroying, any of the Andromedan ships. Huey was no Warrior, he was a Coach, and any injury dismayed him, even an injury to the opposing team. What he hoped to do was frustrate the Andromedans, dazzle them take away the initiative, and demoralize them. Huey believed deeply and fundamentally that a team that didn't think they could win could not win, and he hoped to convince the Andromedans that they could not win.

And so the Top Fifty rolled into the Andromedan fleet like the Hammers of Hell; the linemen and backs braked hard while a hundred tight ends and a hundred wide receivers continued deep, deep into the Andromedans.

Surprise is not the proper word to describe the Andromedan's reaction. They were stupefied as the receivers raced past their fleet. None of them were blocked, and 200 receivers drove past the Andromedan fleet and turned to catch the Beams. No lineman moved to block them; no linebackers, no corner backs, no free safeties, no strong safeties stepped up to intercept the Beams, for, truth be told, the

Andromedans had never heard of Beams, or Space Beam, or Football.

When the Beams were tossed, only fourteen were off the mark, and all but 26 were caught by the receivers. The Andromedan fleet shuddered in the Beam Pattern thrown by 174 Beams, the largest number of Beams ever thrown, hyperdrives switched off, guidance systems went berserk, and the tight, geometric patterns of the Andromedan formation wobbled and broke apart. For hours, even after the Beams shut down and the receivers scrambled back to the line of scrimmage, ready to attack again, the Andromedans tumbled out of control. But, as the Beams first struck, the Voice of the Andromedan equivalent of Huey (Andy?) roared out through the intercoms of both fleets, and into Huey's waiting receivers. It said, roughly,

"By the Great Bodiless Ancient Spirits which Form the Core of Andromedan Culture!"

This Huey translated, very roughly, as

"Great Gosh Almighty!"

"What the hell are you guys *doing*?" it said.

The Head Coach of the Spiral Arm Champion Bills (not that big a coincidence -- 73 teams called themselves "Bills" in 2500 AD, even though no one left alive -- including Huey -- had any idea what a "Bill" was) read a prepared message:

"This is the Head Coach of the Spiral Arm Fleet of the Milky Way Galaxy and you are hereby ordered to stop and make yourselves available for boarding. Please acknowledge your surrender and make ready to receive Spiral Arm personnel who will disarm your vessels and take them under Spiral Arm Control."

She prepared to repeat the message when the Andromedans replied:

"Disarm our vessels? These vessels aren't armed, you Bozo!"

"Uh, not armed?" The Coach stumbled.

"Of course they're not armed! This is a peaceful mission. We've just come to introduce ourselves, and talk about some, uh, *mutual alliances!*" And then the Andromedans added, strangely,

"Take us to your leader!"

This last request caused a lot of problems in the Spiral Arm Fleet, because no one there knew who their leader was, nor were they sure what a leader was. But, in the end, they were torn as to whether it was the Coaches they wanted to see, or Huey, but none of those worthies was what anyone in the fleet thought of as their leader.

Chapter 44: Sorry

OK, OK, I'm sorry. I mean, how could I know that the Andromedan Fleet wasn't a military invasion fleet, but just an outing of horny truckers looking for a little fun during a routine trading mission? I mean, when Uncle Hogg sent me out here to get Earth ready, I naturally assumed he meant ready for *something important*, you know?

Not that I'm sorry there wasn't a war or anything. I'm not a military person myself, and I have no stomach for major violence. Still, it's a pain to have to be Out of Town for twenty thousand years or so just to warn a bunch of locals in one of the Arms that a bunch of rude truck drivers is likely to get fresh with their more attractive citizens!

And I can't say it didn't work out well after all. I mean, if I hadn't put the bug in Huey's ear, Earth would never have gone into space in the big way it did, and it wouldn't have had such a talented group of Spacers, and it wouldn't have formed alliances in 17 other star systems in the Arm, and it wouldn't have had the poop to come out into deep space and put the Andromedans on the floor with that great right cross. They'd remember that punch, you can bet, and it would put them in their place when they arrived for R&R on the Green Hills of Earth. I mean, if Earth hadn't been country tough and ready, these Andromedans could have raised a mighty ruckus, and left a lot of earth boys and girls crying over lost virginity.

As it was, you had a Hell of a Planet, Earth, bustling with enthusiasm, growing like a weed, producing people faster than the no-huddle offense could put points on the scoreboard, colonizing unpopulated planets in seven systems -- a hell of a place, and all because of my visit!

Well, all because of my visit might be a bit much. Actually, human history was always a struggle between conservative and radical forces, and the result was a sort of middle road. But you do have to understand that *Huey blew off every conservative thinker that ever lived* thanks to that sex-crazed maniac Dewey, and, after that, Earth-culture took off like a hot air balloon whose ballast fell off. Everyone who said "no" went away, and the world was left only with those who said "yes." Concepts like "guilt" and "sin" and "patriotism" and "obedience" lost their hold over the population, and the result was an unrestricted outburst of sexuality that would have made the Great God Pan leap for joy (if Huey hadn't inadvertently wiped him away with all the other gods.)

Huey had replaced these regulating devices with the kind of order he knew best: the discipline of professional football. Gods, priests, rabbis, philosophers -- all these went away and were replaced by a single disciplinarian: the coach. The result was a culture that behaved like athletes on the field -- and also behaved like athletes off the field. Understand?

So you won't be surprised that a lot of the players on the Top Fifty teams seemed to like some of the Andromedans. I mean, long-haul space truckers are a pretty tough lot themselves, and you can see how they might appeal to these athletes. Some of the became very close by the time the two fleets rolled into the Green Hills of Earth, now grown even more exciting by the heady news of Victory in Space!

And, one more thing. Now that the Andromedan war, which had occupied Huey's attention for so many centuries, was behind him, Huey turned his complete attention to the discovery of the Meaning of Life. With the same zeal that he had formed the Space Beam Leagues, fostered the development of space travel, honed his battle tactics, prepared his teams and formed the zeal needed to fight off the Andromedans, Huey threw himself into the search.

When the fleet got back, they found an earth that was 750 years older than the battle they had fought less than a year ago (such are the vagaries of relativity). The removal of the Andromedan threat, which had hung over humanity's collective head for nearly 2000 years, along with the great need to produce huge population growth for colonization of the new planetary systems, had brought on a kind of worldwide drunkenness. Freed from a mortal threat, their survival now guaranteed, economic woes not even a memory, new planetary systems to colonize -- humanity turned its collective attentions once again to The Meaning of Life.

When the fleet got back, they found a superheated humanity, freed from all moral and religious constraints, disciplined only by the code of the professional athlete, flushed by victory, hot on the trail of the Meaning of Life, searching the past for the philosophical roots Curly had snatched from them so long ago. And they had the scent in their nostrils -- they knew where it was, and they were digging it out as the first ships landed. For Huey had narrowed his search to a 2000 year old tomb, a tomb in which Earth's finest archaeologists hoped to find the remains of one of the great philosophers and moral leaders of the 20th Century. And in this tomb, Huey hoped to find a clue that would lead him to the Meaning of Life.

Get ready, now, it's nuttier than you think!

Chapter 45: Leon

Quietly at first, then louder and louder they sang, bodies swaying, breasts bursting from loose fabric, pants straining against surging sexual desire beyond all human endurance, genes pressing for expression, humanity surging toward its destiny, individual goals swept aside, humanity stupefied, intelligence gone awry, blood pulsing through distended arteries, mentalities wasted, screaming, bursting, dancing, sweating, singing...

Roll away they stone,
Don't leave me here alone.
Yeah they'll wreck me
And they'll take me.
Don't leave me lyin' here.
What will they do in 2000 years?

And they rolled away the stone.

Inside, Leon was 2000 years of dust, deader than a doornail. Unprotected by the advanced methods of his Egyptian precursors, nothing remained of him that even the science of the Fourth Millennium could identify. But there was...something...there.

Glimmering under 2 millennia of dust, a silver shower of light, dust swept away by intense, unscientific fingers sweeping, caution itself swept aside with the 2000 year old dust, irresponsible, hungry, penile, erect, moist, shimmering, desperate, breathing fast, tearing fingers, ripping out the disk -- a circular, silver disk -- old, old, old, but alive, alive, exciting, glowing, shining -- a disk. Insane, grasping fingers siezing the disk, touching it, hugging it, licking it -- what to do!

Only luck prevented the disk from being smashed into particles as small as the remains of Leon as the passions of the crowd flamed in the face of this new discovery. Huey copied the disk very exactly and sent copies to scientists all over the earth.

But 2000 years is a long time to remember how to read a primitive text, even, or perhaps particularly, one encoded into mathematical pulses burned onto an indestructible plastic disk by primitive laser devices.

One side of the disk was nearly blank, just a shiny silver disk, somewhat duller for the outer two-thirds; inside that a few alternating mirrored and satin-finish silver bands, with a small hole in the exact center. A few words in Earth English were written on that side. One phrase, *Made in USA*, was quickly deciphered, but didn't seem to help much toward The Meaning of Life. Another block of more arcane symbols defied the best experts, and no one ever really determined what *SRZ 8017 03@ AA* meant.

The other side was more promising but more frustrating. It had obviously had some sort of coating on it, but that coating was long since worn away by the same forces that had worn away Leon. But for decades or even centuries, the coating had lasted, and had shielded the disk from erosion where the coating was thickest. Scientists painstakingly recovered much of this information, but, alas, could make little sense of it. Some of the larger letters left enough information to be decoded easily. At the top of the disk, it had said something like (asterisks indicate indecipherable letters)

Shel**er,

and, beneath this, in thicker letters,

Th* B*s* ** L*** Russ***.

The rest of the disk was just a mess. Many much smaller letters seemed to be placed helter-skelter all over the disk. Enough could be recovered to determine that these were numbered phrases, beginning with 1 and (presumably) continuing through 17, but not all of them could be read.

Following each number were phrases, some of which could be made out in part, but none of which made sense. The most nearly complete was the phrase

13. Q**** ** *** R***** Derby (2:24),

but this meant nothing to the scientists. 13, of course, was a major number, complete with mystical meaning, and Derby referred to a kind of hat worn over two thousand years ago. A small industry developed around the recreation of this primitive headgear, and for a long time the cognoscenti went nowhere without the 40th century version of the rounded hats perched on their heads.

In spite of the great popularity of the little round hats, no one came up with a convincing relationship between the dapper beanies and The Meaning of Life. Some experts uncovered ancient records of a kind of contest, called a Derby, where horses competed with each other to circle a kind of oval track in the Southeastern part of the United States as fast as possible, but no one really believed this was the key to the Meaning of Life. What's more, no one could figure out how to get horses to do this, and so a lot of money was lost trying to cash in on this clue.

By far the most exciting clue on the disk (completely misleading, as it turned out) was the phrase

6. Roll A*** *** ***** (3:10),

As the most mush-for-brains reader by now can guess, the word "Roll" was like a firecracker in a truce to Humanity, and everyone immediately counted the letters and assumed (correctly, as it turned out) that it must have meant "Roll Away the Stone", the same song that had led the search for Leon for the last 200 years, the same song Huey had sung as he tore open the tomb where Leon's mortal remains had long ago faded into ashes and dust. This confirmed the collective belief that the silver disk indeed contained a clue to The Meaning of Life.

While this added greatly to the collective lust to decode the silver disk, the Meaning of Life remained an elusive goal.

And so Humanity pondered this puzzle. Huey searched himself for the technical skill; anthropologists skilled in understanding of past cultures turned from passionate beds to study the disk with a different kind of passion. Back and forth from hot, desperate encounters with their fellow investigators, earth's best scrutinized copies of the silver disks. Again and again, deep in passion for their fellow students, scientists tore themselves from hot, sticky, unkempt beds to peruse the strange, silver disks.

As the clues filtered out of the scientific community, tens of thousands of Huey's nodes combined to form hypotheses about The Meaning of Life. By now Huey was convinced the secret was buried in the late 20th Century, and almost all the hypotheses formed around clues from this epoch.

The most common belief, of course, was that the secret lay in Leon. But nothing, not a scrap beside the single chorus of "Roll Away the Stone," remained of Leon's corpus.

And so other clusters formed. The largest and most successful formed under the potent banner of Jagger and Richards, and these were about equally divided among two still existing images. Each marched -- or rolled -- across the green hills of Earth screaming their defining anthems:

You can't always get what you want,

But, if you try sometime,

You just might find

You get what you need!

And, equally popular,

We all need someone to lean on,

And if you want to, Baby,

You can lean on me.

But they were not to prevail. Two main Beatles groups wore them down. The first shouted sweetly

All you need is love, love, love.

All you need is love.

The second chanted

Happiness is a warm, yes it is, GUN!

This second group was buoyed by the corollary phrase, uniting as it did the old religion and the new sexuality, rolled under the powerful banner

Mother Superior Jumped the Gun,

and the combination of these two potent ideas within the same song, added to the Love declarations of the first Beatles cluster, was enough to slow the Stones advance to dominance. (Surprisingly fierce resistance to both these groups formed around an alternative phrase from a cult whose name was thought to be "Raymond" or "Ramen," which asserted "I want to be sedated!", but this group was quite small.)

While these thrusts were enough to prevent the Stones from establishing the foundation of the Meaning of Life for the 40th Century, they were not enough to carry the day for their own views. The reason was simplicity itself: none of these tunes made any reference to the key word, the essential word, the word that New Humanity knew beyond doubt carried the secret to The Meaning of Life, had known for Centuries carried the seed of the human future, the word that, yes, *rolled* off the tongue as the silver disk of Leon would roll down a steep slope, the word

ROLL.

Jagger and Richards were, after all, The *Rolling Stones*. Splinter Beatles groups that held out for the obscure *Roll Over Beethoven* were considered unconvincing. Still, there was a tantalizing clue in this hot Berry number, if only Huey knew what it meant:

Got a little record I want my jockey to play.

If Huey knew what a "record" was, he might have guessed that Leon's silver disk was a CD, and he might have known that none of the copies he had made contained any of the laser pulses which encoded The Meaning of Life onto Leon's silver disk, so that the scientists could study those suckers until hell froze over and never find a thing. And, if nothing else, the word "jockey" might have led him to understand how it was that Old Humanity got those horses to race around the track at the Kentucky Derby.

But Huey hadn't a clue.

Chapter 46: Queenie

They were all right, of course, these hypotheses about the Meaning of Life, or at least right enough. Humanity, dazed and confused, could not ignore the truth. The newly discovered, unpopulated systems in the Arm; communication and transportation lines, for the first time in Milky Way history, yawning open from Earth to the far ends of the Galaxy, Earth, population young, yearning, fertile, hungry, glowing in its acceptance-rejection of the Andromedan suitor, screaming and pulsing to fill the emptiness, driven by the Life Imperative to be fruitful and multiply, unhindered by Confucian and Socratic peons to filial piety and family values, driven to make people, thousands of people, millions and billions of people, people flowing from the Green Hills of Earth, rolling, rolling, *rolling* across the Galaxy...

Huey's Working Hypothesis recognized this truth, as did the surging hormones that rolled through Humanity. Still, there was uncertainty. Humanity thrust itself into the lust for procreation cheerfully and zestfully, but an element of doubt remained. The charge to make love with anyone available might have seemed like a teenager's dream come true. And it was, of course -- let's not overemphasize the little doubts that remained in Huey's collective mind. This was a hell of a good time to be alive. Still, everyone knew that Humanity's understanding of The Meaning of Life was only approximate, and doubts nagged at the collective consciousness. *And why would anyone want to be sedated?*

And this understood, Kween Ee climbed slowly up the decaying stairway of the oldest surviving University on the green hills of Earth. In her hands was Leon's disk. Not a copy of Leon's disk, but the Disk Itself, the very disk that lay covered by the unidentifiable remains of Leon.

Kween Ee did not know that the disks her distinguished colleagues in the rest of the world held were useless junk. She had no idea that The Meaning of Life had nothing to do with the meaningless symbols that were recorded on the surface of the silver circle. She had no concept of what a laser might be, nor did she know that the blank, empty, uninteresting second side of that magnificent disk was inscribed invisibly with Leon's deep understanding of the Nature of Humanity and the Meaning of Life. Like the rest of the Earth's best and brightest, she assumed that the visible symbols were the key.

Kween Ee was not the best or the brightest. Not that she wasn't good or bright, because she was a hell of a bright lady. But the best and brightest of the Green Hills of Earth at that moment was a taxi driver in Des Moines who was bright enough to know that happiness didn't come with great responsibility. What Kween Ee was was one of the most beautiful creatures on Earth in the sex-crazed eyes of the men around her. Fortunately for Kween Ee, however, her childhood in Tulsa, Oklahoma had made her country rough, and she had been able to keep her balance so far.

But she was bright enough. And she had the Disk of Leon because she was Full Professor at the absolutely Number One, Oldest, Most Distinguished University on the Green Hills of Earth -- the University of Buffalo. Buffalo, the Queen City of the Great Lakes, the Pearl of the Green Hills of Earth, the city people would die to live in, Buffalo, the same great city where the Buffalo Bills had rolled over their AFC rivals in the last decade of Leon's Century, only to bow in defeat before the Dallas Cowboys in more Super Bowl's than anyone could imagine.

If someone had told Kween Ee that Leon's generation considered Buffalo the Armpit of the East she would have laughed out loud. Buffalo, that great metropolis of green hills and mighty waters on the shore of Niagara Falls and the mighty Niagara River, where the excited waters of mighty Lake Erie flowed inexorably toward the frigid Lake Ontario, screaming and shouting their arrogance at a sleeping universe...Buffalo! The birthplace of Huey.

Kween Ee would have struggled to understand how the mighty Bills' victories had redefined that Great City in the emerging mind of Humanity, and how the eroding Ozone Layer burned brown spots into the skin of her fellow humans in the infernos of Miami and Atlanta and Houston and Honolulu until the desperate flight of the Really Wealthy had made Buffalo the center of human aspirations and hope. And had made the University of Buffalo the center of human knowledge and the Absolute Center of Consciousness for Humanity. Kween Ee did not know, of course, the role that Huey The Most

Persuasive had played in elevating Buffalo from its unenviable place as the snow capital of the East to the Center of Humanity.

Stretching from Lockport to Erie (and some said Cleveland), Buffalo provided the solitude of deep, snowy winter, unspoiled by salt and sand since the Black & Son Roller Skate had brought about the demise of the once popular automobile, the spectacle of dazzling autumn colors, the sweet reawakening of humanity in Springtime and the deepest, slowest, most languid sleepiness of Summertime. Humanity was happy in Buffalo, and lucky to live there, and cheerful and loving. Truly, Buffalo in 4112 was The City of Good Neighbors.

And the University of Buffalo was its heart, its soul, and its mind -- indeed it was the core of the mind of Huey. Here Huey was strongest, brightest, most conscious, most alert, and most powerful. Buffalo was Huey's home, and Huey loved it here.

But the University of Buffalo's long suit was the past.. Buffalo lived on prestige. In spite of its prominence, Buffalo had nothing like the magnificent modern facilities of the University at Quito, or the super duper new university at Madison, Wisconsin.

And so Kween Ee climbed the decaying staircase to the top floor of the Millard Fillmore Academic Center at the University of Buffalo, walked through the magnificent (but shabby) entrance to the Communication Department, and pressed her thumb to the latch of the Richard A. Holmes Memorial Computer Laboratory.

(Kween Ee had no idea of what a computer might be, nor had she ever heard of the great Richard A. Holmes, whose hardnosed demands for excellence in computing gave the Communication Department at Buffalo the sinew that made it able to survive the bullshit (pardon my French) of the academy for 2000 years. But then neither did Huey. But, as I said, history was Buffalo's strong suit.)

Kween Ee switched on once more the antiquated, underinvested, embarrassingly old equipment of the Richard A. Holmes Memorial

Computer Laboratory, and the antiquated equipment slowly crept into artificial life.

None of this equipment could help Kween Ee, or Huey, and they knew it. But winners don't quit, and quitters don't win, and Kween Ee believed that as much as she believed in the growing tenderness of her tiny nipples.

But, here in the center of Huey's powers, connected to the thrust of Humanity's surging collective consciousness, Kween Ee again felt the creeping fingers of Doubt, a subtle yet powerful intermixing of threads of thought that gnawed at her concupiscence, fought the raging hormones that dulled her own sharp wits. Doubt, that mighty enemy of religion that, in the end, spelled the end of all humanity's great Sacred Truths.

And something else rose also through her private-public mixture of mentality. Something she had seen, something she remembered. Of course!

"Wait!", she snapped. "Wait a minute!"

Kween Ee turned from her new Andromedan friend's hot hands and skated toward the door, with him in quick pursuit. He was a hell of a good looking man, and no woman could ignore him. Just one look from his piercing grey-green eyes made her whole body melt into the floor. She daydreamed for a few seconds of how wonderful it would feel to have his strong arms around her, embraced in a gentle but passionate kiss, his hands caressing and massaging first her back then slowly moving down to her buttocks. She with one hand holding the back of his neck, occasionally pulling gently on the brown curls that fell loosely between her fingers -- the other hand massaging his hips, and then, with both hands, pushing his pelvis closer to hers...

But she had a nagging feeling that wouldn't go away. She loved his hands on her skin but she wasn't sure she loved *him*. I mean, she was, God knew, Extremely Horny, and his hands made her tingle, but there was something about her that didn't ... didn't ... want ... *him*.

She covered the mile from Fillmore in about a minute, then skated up the magnificent marble stairway to the Lockwood Memorial Library, passed the waiting elevators and on up the next flight of stairs to the Most Sacred room on the University's hallowed campus. Hands shaking she swung open the door and began to undo the seals on the Inner Sanctum of Leon Hall. Quickly she ran to the sealed glass case and spoke the commands that switched on the protective fields around the case. Slowly, incredibly slowly the case lifted.

The Andromedan had followed more slowly, but now his hand once again slid gently onto her shoulder, and Kween Ee again felt the warmth surging through her body and dulling her mind. God, the Andromedans were a good-looking bunch, and Kween EE, like everyone else on earth, was dazed by the new sexual imperative to reproduce as many new humans as possible, even if some of them might be half Andromedan. But the Doubt was too great now for mere hormones, and her eyes darted quickly through the display until they riveted onto the black device that had flashed into her mind's eye one mile away in Fillmore.

If the device hadn't been there, Kween Ee might have rolled over onto her back and let the Andromedan do what he wanted (and, maybe, maybe, she wanted too, but she wasn't ... wasn't ... *sure*.) But it was there.

With a deep reverence she reached toward the device and touched it with a gentleness she hadn't felt in her lifetime. She scarcely felt the trembling hands that slipped forward over her neck and slid tentatively across her chest onto her breast. Her hormones had already driven her to the point of insanity, and the warmth of the Andromedan hands were more than anyone could have resisted under more normal circumstances. But her eyes were fixed on the ancient inscription on that inscrutable device:

Discman.

And this word saved her. Of course! Look at the size of it, the name, so obvious, how could I have taken so long to see it? she thought. Her hand touched the rounded rectangle on the left front corner of the top where the inviting, welcoming, promising word beckoned her:

Open

and, with a snap, the lid lifted, and the truth was so obvious she laughed out loud.

Quickly but reverently she slipped the shining silver disk into the Discman. She stared at the disk as it clicked positively into what was clearly its proper place, the place it wanted to be more than any other. Slowly, almost with regret, she pressed the lid closed, and her hand moved toward the largest button on the device almost as the invading Andromedan hand moved toward a smaller, softer button between her legs.

The Discman had lain in Leon Hall at the Lockwood Library for 800 years, after it had been discovered, curiously preserved in a box buried on the shore of a small lake in Northeastern Oklahoma. Technicians at the University of Buffalo had studied the device for a long time, and restored it as nearly as they could, but since no one knew what it was or what it did, no one knew if it actually worked or not.

But the Discman did work, or at least it almost worked. It's primitive silicon mind failed to understand much of the decoding information at the beginning of the disk, but it stumbled on valiantly, skipping the first dozen tracks on the ancient disk, hovering briefly over the 13th item, skipped ahead by an unbelievably fortuitous few bits -- *and began to track.*

And Leon's sweet whisky voice sang out, cheerfully, rhythmically, rolling across the ancient message of the long gone Steinway Model D, supported by a choir of angelic voices, The Meaning of Life.

As the words rolled from the tiny Discman speakers into Kween EE's own mind, and from there to Huey and the rest of humanity, she felt the uncontrollable beginnings of a feeling she only dimly remembered from the Andromeda War, a feeling buried in the deepest recesses of the collective brain stem, a feeling that rises anew in the human breast as needed. Kween Ee felt the fingers of her right hand curling involuntarily, felt the soft muscles of her forearm turning to steel, felt her arm pull back, the muscles in her chest tightening with a will of their own, her clenched fist cocking as the Great Leon repeated, over and over again on the malfunctioning Discman, the immortal words of The Meaning of Life:

Remember the time when a trucker from Dallas
Was callous to Queenie with his rude sighs.
No one can deny that he got much more than he bargained for.
Queenie's right cross brought him to the floor.
Now he knows better
Than to mess with the Queen of the Roller Derby,
The Queen of the Roller Derby

Author's Note

This book tells a story about an Assistant Professor of Communication at the University at Buffalo and an unemployed computer engineer, a bicycle vendor, and a Little Richard imitator who upgrade a commercial software package (Galileo) so that it becomes a collective planet-wide intelligence. The Milky Way Galaxy sends another collective intelligence to offer assistance, which leads to an intergalactic football game between the Andromeda galaxy and the Milky Way. In the end, we reveal the Meaning of Life.

The main characters names are Hui, Dewey and Lu Wi, Curly, Larry and Mao. There's a dipstick whose name may be Roscoe, whose Boss is named Hogg. Larry so improves roller skates that they replace automobiles. There are innumerable Queens, including a Queen of old China, the Queen City of the Great Lakes (Buffalo, NY), the Queen of Rock and Roll, and a 40th Century scientist name Kween EE, and, in the end, the Queen of the Roller Derby. So it almost goes without saying (Duh!) that this is a work of fiction, and any resemblance to any person living would be better off dead (with apologies to Red Skelton).

So please understand that I mean no ill will to the great University at Buffalo, State University of New York, which is an excellent university destined for greatness. And I certainly mean no harm to the great Department of Communication at that institution, which I believe to be the foremost scientific communication department in the world. It also has a sense of humor, which is part of why it's great.

Dean Kurland is a complete work of fiction, not to be confused with any of the deans and deanlets at the College of Arts and Science (CAS) at the University at Buffalo where the Communication Department actually resides. CAS is my favorite college, ever, and a model of how a major college in a major public research university ought to be run.

As far as I know there has never been a rhetorician as chair of the UB Communication Department, which is the single most scientific department of communication in the world. All the chairs of the communication department have been crazy, however, which is a tradition I hope will go on. If there is any hope that the discipline of communication will prove, in the end, to have some positive impact on our understanding of the world, I believe it is the UB communication department that will lead the way.

And as for the City of Buffalo, don't believe a word I've said. Go on thinking of it as a cold, unpleasant place, just as Johnny Carson said it was. First Prize, one week in Buffalo. Second Prize, two weeks in Buffalo. Stay in Atlanta or Phoenix or Los Angeles. Don't come here. If too many people find out about the mild climate, the very pleasant summers, the uncrowded streets and highways, the low cost of housing, the tremendous multicultural food, restaurants, festivals, the major art and theater, the intellectual benefits of the flagship campus of the State University of New York (with the largest percentage of international students of any public university in America), the Buffalo Philharmonic Orchestra, Kleinhans Music Hall, one of the most amazing venues in the world, the jazz and folk scene, quick and easy access to our fabulous Canadian neighbors, and, above all, the willingness of people to talk to each other, as befits the City of Good Neighbors -- hey, many people might move here and, next thing you know, it's noisy, grouchy, overpriced and unpleasant like so many other American cities.

The technology, however, is real, and, within the limits of poetic license, the descriptions of that technology are accurate. You can Google Galileo, Catpac ThoughtView, Spot and Rover and find it all there. You can even find hundreds of scientific papers if you Google Galileo Literature.

www.ingramcontent.com/pod-product-compliance
Lightning Source LLC
Chambersburg PA
CBHW061508020726
47502CB00006B/1989